WHAT MOMMA LEFT ME

An ABC New Voices Pick

PIECING ME TOGETHER

Newbery Honor Book · Coretta Scott King Author Award
Los Angeles Times Book Prize, Young Adult Finalist
A New York Public Library Best Book for Teens
A Chicago Public Library Best Book, Teen Fiction
An ALA Top Ten Best Fiction for Young Adults
An NPR Best Book · A *Kirkus Reviews* Best Teen Book
A Refinery29 Best Book

"Timely and timeless." —Jacqueline Woodson

"Brilliant." —John Green

"About what impacts young women today." —Meg Medina

"Watson writes with rhythm and style." —Jason Reynolds

"It will linger with you." —Bustle

"Reminds us that love between elders and youth
is worth the work." —*Ebony*

★ "Teeming with compassion and insight."
—*Publishers Weekly*, starred review

★ "A timely, nuanced, and unforgettable story
about the power of art, community, and friendship."
—*Kirkus Reviews*, starred review

THIS SIDE OF HOME

"Watson is a master of discovery and healing the heart."
—Naomi Shihab Nye

★ "Thoughtful, powerful." —*BCCB*, starred review

★ "Essential for all collections." —*Booklist*, starred review

"Readers get a rich, thoughtful, and deeply engaging story
that they'll be talking about for much, much longer than it
takes them to get to the final page." —Bustle

WHAT
MOMMA
LEFT ME

Books by Renée Watson

What Momma Left Me
This Side of Home
Piecing Me Together
Watch Us Rise (coauthored with Ellen Hagan)

WHAT
MOMMA
LEFT ME

RENÉE WATSON

BLOOMSBURY
NEW YORK LONDON OXFORD NEW DELHI SYDNEY

BLOOMSBURY YA
Bloomsbury Publishing Inc., part of Bloomsbury Publishing Plc
1385 Broadway, New York, NY 10018

BLOOMSBURY and the Diana logo are trademarks of Bloomsbury Publishing Plc

First published in the United States of America in July 2010
by Bloomsbury Children's Books
Original paperback edition published in March 2012
New edition published in January 2019 by Bloomsbury YA

Bloomsbury books may be purchased for business or promotional use.
For information on bulk purchases please contact Macmillan Corporate and
Premium Sales Department at specialmarkets@macmillan.com

ISBN 978-1-68119-949-8 (paperback) · ISBN 978-1-5476-0173-8 (hardcover)
ISBN 978-1-59990-594-5 (e-book)

The Library of Congress has cataloged the hardcover edition as follows:
Watson, Renée.
What Momma left me / by Renée Watson. — 1st U.S. ed.
p.   cm.
Summary: After the death of their mother, thirteen-year-old
Serenity Evans and her younger brother go to live with their grandparents,
who try to keep them safe from bad influences and help them come to
terms with what has happened to their family.
ISBN 978-1-59990-446-7 (hardcover)
[1. Grief—Fiction. 2. Family problems—Fiction. 3. Grandparents—Fiction.
4. Christian life—Fiction. 5. Orphans—Fiction.
6. African Americans—Fiction.] I. Title.
PZ7.W32868Wh 2010   [Fic]—dc22   2009018263

Book design by Jeanette Levy
Typeset by Westchester Publishing Services
Printed and bound in the U.S.A. by Berryville Graphics Inc., Berryville, Virginia
2 4 6 8 10 9 7 5 3 1

All papers used by Bloomsbury Publishing Plc are natural, recyclable products
made from wood grown in well-managed forests. The manufacturing processes
conform to the environmental regulations of the country of origin.

To find out more about our authors and books visit www.bloomsbury.com
and sign up for our newsletters.

For my mother,
Carrie Elizabeth Watson,
the definition of resilience

WHAT
MOMMA
LEFT ME

OUR FATHER

. . . .

I don't have many good memories of my daddy.
He was hardly home.
And when he was,
he was mad
at my momma,
or me,
or my younger brother, Danny.
Always yelling about what wasn't done right,
what wasn't done at all,
what he was going to do.
He bought me gifts though.
Always on Christmas, on Valentine's Day, and
on my birthday.
He gave me this diary two months ago, when I
turned thirteen.

I never thought about writing in it until now.
I need a place to put these secrets.
They're too heavy for me to carry alone.

Grandma says I am just like my momma. She says I look like her, talk like her, act like her. My chocolate eyes, crayon-brown skin, and skinny, knock-kneed legs are the same as my momma's when she was my age. "Serenity, girl, if I didn't know better I'd think this was a picture of my Loretta," Grandma says, holding up my school photo. I think she is sad but also glad that even though she can't see her own child anymore, she can always look at me.

Danny, my brother, looks like my daddy—tall, dark skinned, and skinny no matter how much he eats. He is one year younger than me. He'll be starting the seventh grade. I'm starting the eighth. I don't mind us being just like our parents on the outside. But I'm scared that maybe we're like them on the inside too.

Danny has my daddy's temper. Just yesterday, he punched the wall because he couldn't find his hat. He was mad at me, thinking I hid it. He made a mess looking for it—clothes thrown all over the floor. Then he remembered that he had put it in the closet. Busted knuckles for nothing.

Danny also has my daddy's style—expensive, name-brand shoes, baggy jeans, oversized shirts. Momma always said, "Boy, you're a carbon copy of your father." She never sounded happy when she said it.

Sometimes I wonder if all children are like their parents. I think about having a different momma and a different daddy. I think, maybe if I wasn't the daughter of Loretta and Daniel Evans Sr. everything that happened this summer would change.

But I am Serenity Evans and nothing can change that.

I think sometimes my daddy wants everything to change too. I know he doesn't like being a father. He's never said it, but I just know. I know because there are no pictures of him holding me when I was a baby. I know because he never came to any of my school plays or recitals. He is always gone—running the streets, my momma would say. She made excuses for him, trying to convince us that he really did care, but I think even she stopped believing her lies.

I think Momma realized that no matter how many good qualities there are in my daddy, there are more bad. One night when I woke up thirsty, I got out of bed to get a drink of water. I stopped just before I got to the kitchen when I saw my daddy and my brother, Danny, sitting at the kitchen table. They were stuffing small plastic bags with green plants. Daddy said, "One day, Lil Shorty, I'll take you out with me and show you how *this* green brings you *this* green." He took a wad of money out of his pocket and tossed it on the table. Danny picked up the bills in amazement.

I turned around and went back to bed. I never told anyone. I knew my momma would just cuss and fuss at my dad and then he'd get mad and they'd fight. Then my dad would leave for a few a days, like he always does after they fight—to give my mom some space and clear his head, he says. Whenever Momma would question him about where he was staying, he'd tell her as long as the rent was paid she didn't need to worry about it. And they'd argue again and he'd leave, so I just kept my mouth shut about Danny helping my daddy.

I'm really good at keeping secrets. I still haven't told any of my momma's.

I know better than to tell these things to anybody. No good would come of it. And besides, Momma always told me not to go telling our family's business. "What happens in this house, stays in this house," she'd always say.

Not anymore.

Now that momma's gone, our secrets are getting out and our house is empty because two kids can't live alone. And this is another reason why I know my dad doesn't care about us. I know because he hasn't come home. I don't even know if he knows my momma is dead. I wonder what he will do when he comes home to an empty house.

WHICH

. . . .

Grandma Mattie wants us.
I do not like her.
She is my daddy's mother.
Her house has no pictures of my momma.
She tells the social worker
there's room for us at her place.
But we want to live with
Grandpa James and Grandma Claire.
They are my momma's parents.
Their house is full of pictures of our momma.

I haven't been back to the house since my momma died.
At first, I am scared to go in, but once Grandpa James's
car pulls up and we see that the news and neighbors and

strangers are all gathered around the house waiting for us, I just want to run inside. Grandpa stops and talks to some of them. There are reporters from the *Portland Observer* and the *Oregonian* scribbling in their tablets as Grandpa speaks. "My family would like to thank the Portland community for your prayers and support. We appreciate your kindness." For the past three days people have been sending food, flowers, cards, and money to Grandpa James and Grandma Claire's house. Especially people from Restoration Baptist Church, where my grandpa is the pastor. My momma grew up in that church, but by the time she had me she stopped going.

Grandma walks past the crowd, grabbing us by our hands, squeezing mine tight, and rushes us to the house. Grandma's hands are soft and her nails are always painted with clear nail polish. She dresses in the nicest clothes and sometimes she lets me play in her soft, wooly hair. I like to comb through the silver and black strings, braid them, and see the new patterns the gray makes.

Grandma is a big woman. Wide hips and thick legs. She says it's from having babies and cooking all those good family recipes. Grandma says cooking and baking is a family heirloom passed down from her mother's mother. She caters for weddings and all kinds of special events. My momma cooked too. Momma promised me that one day she'd teach me how to make a red velvet cake and all the other secret family recipes, but now that she's gone, she can't.

Grandma squeezes my hand tighter the closer we get to the door. Even though my momma always entered the house through the side door, we go in the front. I am glad I don't have to walk into the kitchen.

"You two just need to pack enough clothes for the week. Your grandpa and I will come back later for everything else," Grandma tells us. "And bring your games too," she says, eyeing Danny's video games and controllers. They are scattered on the floor in the living room. I remember that the day my momma died, Danny was sitting on the living room floor, with his back against the bottom of the sofa, playing video games. The TV was loud, as if the war on the screen was happening in our living room. I remember my momma telling me to tell Danny to turn the game off.

"Serenity, honey, did you hear me?" Grandma taps me on my shoulder and I shake the picture out of my head and look at her. "I asked you where the suitcases are kept," she repeats.

"In the closet in my momma's room," I tell her. Grandma walks down the hallway to my parents' room. When she walks inside, she starts weeping. I turn the television on because I don't like the sounds of her sadness.

The news is on and a picture of my momma, the one taken of her last Christmas, is showing on the screen. A reporter says, "Loretta Evans will be laid to rest Thursday morning—"

That's all I hear because Grandma comes in the living room and snatches the remote out of my hand. She turns the TV off. "I don't want you watching the news! You hear me?" She is asking me questions but I know I am not supposed to answer. I don't know why Grandma is yelling at me and why she doesn't want me to see the news. I already know the things they are going to say. "No TV, you understand? No TV unless I am in the room!" Grandma is yelling and crying and I start to cry too. Not because she is yelling at me, but because I am not used to seeing her this way.

"Sorry, Grandma." My voice must sound like I feel— scared and confused.

Grandma takes my hand. She looks down at me and says, "Serenity, I didn't mean to yell at you. I—I just don't want you and Danny seeing those images over and over again."

"But, Grandma, the news has nothing to do with it," I tell her. "I see those images all the time in my dreams."

Grandma looks at me, tears in her eyes, and for the first time in her whole life I think she doesn't know what to say.

Grandpa comes in the house. He is just as wide as Grandma, but taller. "What's that for?" he asks Grandma. And then I notice that Grandma has one of my momma's dresses folded across her arm. The white one she bought two weeks ago. She thought it cost too much but decided to buy it anyway. To treat herself, she said, as we walked to the checkout. Then, when the cashier rang it up, we found out it was on sale. Momma was so happy she bought herself a matching purse.

"I'll dress her tomorrow," Grandma says. "For the casket."

I don't know why, but I am really angry when I hear this. Angry that my momma has been in the same clothes for three days. I go to my room and pack my clothes. Even though Grandma said to only pack for a week, I put in extra. Just in case something happens.

"Serenity?" Danny knocks on the door just as I zip my overnight bag. His eyes are red and puffy from crying; he talks like all his energy has run away. Like when he was sick last winter with the flu.

"Huh?"

"Should I take my Goldfish?"

"What?"

"My crackers for snack time. Should I take them?"

"If you want to," I say.

Danny just stands there. "Will you get them for me?"

I look at him, standing there. "Where's Grandma?"

"Taking my suitcase to the car," he answers.

"Where's Grandpa?"

"Helping Grandma make room in the trunk," Danny says.

I turn the light out and close the door. "Come on," I say. We walk toward the kitchen. Danny is behind me. The closer I get to the kitchen, the more my heart beats my insides. My stomach flips upside down and my hands are sweating. I remember feeling like this last Halloween when Danny and I went trick or treating with our cousins Brian and Michael.

The woman who lives in the house at the end of the block had a fake coffin in her yard and played a recording of scary noises howling through the bushes. I was scared to go up to the door, but I did it anyway. I wanted the candy.

But this is different. I don't want to be brave. I want Danny to say that he doesn't care about the Goldfish crackers that Momma bought him for his snack. But instead he says in a small voice, "They'll get stale if we don't eat them."

And I remember how mad my daddy got when the milk spoiled because we hadn't drank it fast enough. He made my momma drink it. "Ain't no wastin' food in this house!" Daddy kept screaming as he forced the glass of milk to her mouth. Momma got sick and we were careful never to waste food again.

I walk to the end of the living room and stand in the dining room. The kitchen will be next. Grandpa comes inside. "Your grandma's waiting in the car. You two ready?" he asks.

I look at Danny. He says, "Can you get my snack crackers from the pantry?"

Grandpa looks at us. "You want anything else?"

We shake our heads.

Grandpa goes into the kitchen without hesitation, like a superhero. I hear him rummaging through the pantry and then the cabinet door slams shut. "Sure you don't need something else?"

Then I think to ask for one more thing. "Can you bring me the plaque?"

"What plaque?"

"The prayer that hangs over the stove. Do you see it?"

I hear Grandpa strain as he reaches for it, and I feel bad for asking an old man to work so hard. Grandma says he needs to take it easy since his heart attack last year. Grandpa comes out of the kitchen with a box of Goldfish crackers in one hand and the plaque in the other. The plaque is a thick square, dark brown trimmed in gold. Centered in the middle of the brown is a shiny gold square with black writing. The top of the plaque says *The Lord's Prayer* and under it the scripture is printed in fancy writing.

Our Father which art in heaven,
hallowed be thy name.
Thy kingdom come. Thy will be done,
in earth, as it is in heaven.
Give us this day our daily bread.
And forgive us our debts,
as we forgive our debtors.
And lead us not into temptation,
but deliver us from evil:

For thine is the kingdom, and the power,
and the glory, forever. Amen.

The day Momma died, the only thing that made me feel better was saying that prayer. Momma said it whenever she was sad and lonely, so that day I stood in the kitchen, holding Danny's hand, and read the prayer over and over out loud until help came.

"Thank you," Danny and I say. Danny takes the crackers. He opens the box and starts eating them like they are the best thing he's ever tasted. I take the plaque, holding it tight. Grandpa turns off the lights and we leave.

"You two don't have to be afraid. You're safe with me," Grandpa says. "And, ah, we can go grocery shopping to get you some more snacks when those run out." We get into the car. I love Grandpa for this and I am glad he told the social worker that he wanted me and Danny because I want him too.

As we drive away, I think maybe we should have left a note for my dad. But I'm sure he'll know where to find us. Grandma turns and looks at us from the front seat. "Sweethearts, put your seat belts on." She sees the plaque in my hand and smiles. "Your mother's favorite scripture," she says. I read it to myself again and again the whole way to my new home.

· · · · · · ·

Momma's funeral is over and I am glad. I hated sitting at that church, in the front row, right in front of her casket. I hated the songs, the scriptures, the crying, the people telling me I would be okay. I hated the way Danny screamed when they opened the casket. The way he cried so hard, he slept all afternoon because he was too tired to do anything else. I hated the way my momma looked—like clay, like Play-Doh. I hated that she looked happy and peaceful, like she was glad she was gone. Like not living was what she wanted. I will never go to a funeral again and if I have to, I will not look in the casket. It is unfair that the dead have smiles on their faces and the living are left crying.

"Serenity! Danny!" Grandma shouts. "Come here, please," she says. Danny and I walk into the kitchen. "Your grandfather and I want to talk with you."

I sit down next to Danny, across from Grandma. Grandpa is sitting at the head of the table. He clears his throat. "Your grandma and I have thought about this, and we think it'll be best for all of us if you and Danny transfer from Eagle Creek to Rose City Academy."

"Do we have to?" I ask.

Grandma says, "Yes, sweetheart. It's closer to the house. This way, if me or your grandfather can't pick you up, you two can walk home."

"But all my friends go to Eagle Creek." I can't believe I'm finally in the eighth grade and won't be able to take advantage of this. At Rose City it won't matter that I'm an eighth grader, I'll be the new girl.

"Rose City Academy is a good school," Grandma says. "It'll get you prepared for high school." I can tell Grandma chose her words carefully. I know what she really means. Eagle Creek Middle School is always in the news and the paper because our test scores are low. "And there are no uniforms at Rose City Academy," she says.

Her tactic works on Danny. "Good," he says. "Those blue and white uniforms at Eagle Creek are ugly."

Grandma keeps listing reasons why Rose City Academy is a good school (trying to convince me), and finally she says in a soft voice, "We think it will be good for you to start over."

Start over. Maybe she's right. At a new school, I could avoid all the questions and the sad looks that people keep giving me because they know about my momma. At a new school, with new teachers and new friends, I can just be Serenity. Not Serenity who looks like her mother, Loretta. No one will know. Danny and I can just be.

"What about Daddy?" Danny asks.

Grandpa leans back in his chair. "What about him?"

"Will he know where we are? How is he going to find us when he comes back?"

Grandpa looks each of us in the eye, then speaks. "I don't think your father is coming back."

"Why?" I ask.

"It's been a week. Don't you think he would have contacted us by now?" Grandpa asks. It gets real quiet. The ticking of the clock is the only noise I hear.

Danny looks at me. I don't know what to say. It must be true. Most of the time Grandpa is right.

ART IN HEAVEN

· · · · · · · · · ·

I dream of her being in heaven.
No more bruises.
No more pain.
She is the prettiest angel there.
She has wings like the others,
but Momma doesn't fly.
She just sits at Jesus' feet
'cause they haven't talked in a while.

I like living at Grandpa James and Grandma Claire's
house. So many things are different here. Every house
on the block is nice. All the yards are neat and there is
no tall grass spilling over to the next-door neighbor's
yard. There are no raggedy cars that don't work parked

in front of the houses and there are more houses than apartments or duplexes.

Danny and I share a room upstairs. There's a bathroom next to our room and across the hallway is Grandpa's home office. We don't know what to do with all this space. There is enough room for us to be on our own side and not even touch each other. My bed is on the right side of the room, against the wall, near a window. I pull the string to the blinds and let the sun come in.

"We should paint," Danny says. "This is a girl color."

"Yellow is not just for girls."

"Yes it is." Danny starts unpacking the rest of his clothes. We each have our own dresser. There's a big closet that we'll divide, and I think I'd like to hang some posters on the wall. Danny says, "We should paint it white. White is for boys and girls."

"Well, I'm not asking. You ask," I tell Danny.

"Fine," he says. He closes the drawer and starts to make his bed.

Grandma and Grandpa call us down for dinner. A big pot of spaghetti is on the stove and garlic bread is in the oven. After dinner we watch TV and finish unpacking. We are both so tired, Grandma doesn't even have to tell us to get ready for bed.

I get into bed first. When Danny is finished taking his bath, he comes into the bedroom, turns off the light, and gets into his bed. "Serenity?"

"Yes?"

"Do you think Grandpa is right about Daddy?"

"I don't know." I pull the covers over me and try to go to sleep.

"He's been gone longer than a week before," Danny says.

I sit up in the bed. "Do you want Daddy to come back for us?"

I can barely hear Danny's answer. "Sometimes."

I don't say anything.

"I just want to tell him about Momma. Make sure he knows."

"And then what?" I ask.

"I don't know."

"Do you want to live with him?" I ask.

"No," Danny says without hesitating. "I just want to know if he knows about Momma."

I lie back down.

"It's only been a week. Last time he left, he was gone for four, remember?"

"Yeah, I remember," I say. I turn over on my stomach.

Danny falls asleep.

The house is quiet and I can hear Grandma and Grandpa moving around downstairs. They go into their bedroom and close the door. They must not know that their voices rise through the vent. Whenever I am in our room I can hear everything that's being said downstairs. I hear my grandma say, "James, I never thought I'd have to bury one of our children." I can tell she's crying. Now that Momma is gone, Grandpa and Grandma only have two children. Uncle Brian and Aunt Sara.

Grandpa says, "We're going to be okay, honey. We're going to be okay."

They are quiet for a long time. Too long. I don't like it when it's this quiet. My grandma is sniffing. "You should have Pastor Mitchell take over service for the next few Sundays."

"Yeah," Grandpa says. "Don't feel much like preaching." He sighs, then sobs come. "Help us, Father. Help us," he prays.

I bury my head in my pillow, plugging my ears, like I used to do when my parents would fight. I don't know which is worse, falling asleep listening to my momma and my daddy yell and argue, or my grandparents pray and weep.

I thought that one good thing about living with Grandpa and Grandma would be no more sleepless nights.

• • • • • • •

When morning comes, Grandma calls us down for breakfast. She's baked biscuits, scrambled eggs, and fried ham in a skillet. Neither of them looks like they were crying last night. We sit down and eat.

"Slow down, Danny," Grandma says. "That food's not going anywhere."

We laugh.

"It's good," Danny says. He grabs another biscuit from the basket in the middle of the table.

Grandpa takes a sip of his coffee and opens the newspaper. He closes it real fast and sets it on the table. Grandma says, "I read it earlier. Nothing new." And I know there must be an article about my momma in the paper. And probably a picture too. And I get real mad. Mad that people are writing about my momma. Telling our secrets.

Grandma gets up from the table and begins to put the dishes in the dishwasher. "Serenity, I'm cooking your favorite for dinner tonight—teriyaki chicken wings and macaroni and cheese. Guess we should add a vegetable in there, huh? You want to help?"

"No."

"But, Serenity, baby, you love to cook. You sure you don't want to help?"

"No, not tonight."

"You want to help make dessert? I'm thinking about making a red velvet cake."

"No!" I yell. I don't know why I am screaming and how these tears have come with no warning. "I don't want to help you cook! I don't want to help you bake! I don't want to be sitting here in this stupid kitchen with you!" I leave the kitchen, go to my bedroom, and slam the door. Danny follows me upstairs. He's crying too. Lately, he cries if I cry and I start up when he's upset. We've cried so much this past week, sometimes I think we'll use up all our tears. Danny goes into Grandpa's office.

I am sure Grandma is coming for us. She knows we're sad, but she does not allow screaming and slamming doors in her house. I know I will be in trouble for this. The tears streaming down my face are hot and all I want is to go back to the day my momma died. I want to go back to the moments right before and stay there.

I hear footsteps and think Grandma has come to fuss at me, but instead it's Grandpa and he goes into his office. I hear Grandpa tell Danny everything is going to be fine and that it's okay to cry. My daddy would disagree. He always told Danny to be a man, to never let anyone see him cry. One day when we were in elementary school, Danny fell off his bike. His knee was bleeding, and dirt and all kinds of small rocks got into the wound. The edges of his hands, right at his wrists, were scratched up and bleeding too, and my daddy asked him what he was crying for.

"You better man up! Stop all that cryin'. You a man, right?" Daddy used to tell Danny that if he didn't stop crying he was going to give him something to cry for. And here Grandpa is telling him it is okay to cry. "Go ahead, let it out," I hear Grandpa say. "If you don't, you'll be letting it out in other ways."

Danny whispers, "I miss her."

"I know. I do too." Grandpa and Danny go outside. Their voices trail off toward the back of the house. I think

Grandpa is showing Danny the car he is working on. He works on old cars in his garage. Danny's been helping him since he was old enough to pass tools.

The rest of the day goes by and I don't go down for dinner. I end up sleeping right past it. I think Grandma lets me stay asleep because she knows I have been having nightmares and losing sleep lately. I wake up in the middle of the night. Danny is snoring in the other bed. The sound of his soft purrs puts me right back to sleep.

· · · · · · ·

Summer is going by faster than I thought it would. Sometimes the days drag on, but now it's the last weekend before school starts. The calendar that Danny hung on our bedroom wall is all marked up with Xs across each date. Four weeks have passed since my momma died. One month and my father still hasn't come for us. I'm starting to think that maybe my daddy does know about my mom. I think maybe he just doesn't care.

Danny swears he's not counting anymore. He says he never was. He says he was counting down the days till school started. Danny's never been excited about school, so I know that's a lie.

He's never been excited about church either. And so every Sunday morning it's like trying to get a hibernating bear to wake up. "Rise and shine!" Grandma says, knocking on our bedroom door. It's Sunday morning and it's time to get ready for church. We've been to church more this summer than in my whole life. We go to church every Sunday—*all* day, and sometimes on weeknights too, if there's a special service or meeting. We also go on Saturday mornings. It seems like we'll be in church just as much as we'll go to school. And Grandpa says that's good. There is nothing more important than having God and education in your life, he says. With Grandpa being a pastor and Grandma a retired teacher there is no way we will fail at faith or academics.

Grandma sings in the choir, teaches Bible study, and is the organizer and head cook for the church's soup kitchen. That is why we are always at church. There is always a rehearsal, a meeting, a time of prayer, a Bible study, a youth group, a community service activity. Always something.

Danny does not like this, but I do. At church, I like the singing and I like reciting the memory verses. Grandma is impressed that I can memorize scriptures so well. She says that I should have no problem at my Rites of Passage—a ceremony where all the youth of the church are passed to the next level of leadership training. At the end of eighth grade I will be eligible to become a Teen Disciple. In order to move up to a Teen Disciple, I have to write a statement of faith, recite a passage of scripture, and complete a community service project. I'm thinking maybe one of my projects will have something to do with art. I've been liking all the art projects we do in Sunday school class.

We make art pieces inspired by the stories we learn in class. We've learned how to do printmaking and ceramics. Sometimes we draw or paint or make collages. Once I used Cray-Pas to illustrate Moses and the burning bush—oranges, reds, yellows, black smoke. Using water-colors, I painted Joseph and his coat of many colors—blues, purples, greens.

Today, we're not doing art. Miss Valerie, our Sunday school teacher, is standing at the front of the room with a DVD in her hand. "Okay, class," Miss Valerie says. "We're going to watch a video today." Miss Valerie goes to the DVD player and puts in a disk.

"This better be good!" I hear a girl say. I turn around and see a girl the color of caramel sitting behind me. Her jet black hair is long and curly. It looks like the kind that doesn't nap up when it gets wet. She moves my sweater from the empty chair next to me and slides her thin body through the row of chairs so she can sit beside me. "You know what I'm saying?" she continues. "This better not be about obeying our parents or saying no to drugs." She rolls her eyes and crosses her legs. "You're Pastor James's granddaughter, right?"

"Yes. My name is Serenity."

"I'm Maria," she says.

"You go to church here?" I ask.

"Yeah. I've been gone all summer visiting my grand-parents in Mexico," she tells me. That explains her hair. "You know what this video is about?"

"No," I say.

"Well, why not? You a PK, so you should know everything."

"A PK?"

"Preacher's Kid," Maria says. "Or in your case, grand-kid." She looks very disappointed. "Your mom and dad go here too?" she asks.

"No," I tell her. "I don't have parents."

"Everybody has parents," Maria says.

"Not me," I tell her. She looks at me like she wants an explanation. A reason. I can't tell the truth. Not to some girl I just met, not in the middle of a Sunday school class.

"Well, do you have any brothers or sisters?" Maria asks.

"One brother," I say. I point to Danny.

Maria looks him over.

"He's a year younger than me," I tell her.

"I'm an only child. Just me and my mom," Maria says. "Well, and my dad. But he doesn't live with us. He lives in Vancouver." Maria digs in her purse and pulls out a pack of gum. She puts the watermelon-flavored square in her mouth and chews. "Want some?"

I take a piece, even though I know we aren't supposed to chew gum in church.

"So, for real," Maria says. "Where does your dad live?"

My palms start to sweat. "Northeast Portland."

"You see him a lot?"

I tell the lie I heard my momma say to nosy people who'd ask her a bunch of questions about where my dad was. "He's out of town on business a lot," I say. I wonder where my dad really is. At home, every time the phone rings I think maybe it's him calling to say he's back. Calling to see where we are. But it never is.

Maria continues with the questioning. "What about your mom? How come you don't live with her?"

I bite my lip. "My mom died in a car accident," I lie.

Maria gives me those sad eyes everybody kept giving me at the funeral. "I'm sorry. I didn't know."

"It's okay," I lie again. I push out the memories I have of the day my momma died and I swallow the truth and keep my momma's secrets buried on the inside.

Miss Valerie stands at the front of the room. "Before we begin, class, I just want to remind everyone that there's no gum chewing in church."

Two girls and a boy spit their gum out in the garbage can. I slide mine to the back of my mouth, on the right side.

Miss Valerie turns the lights off. The DVD starts and a voice comes on that says, "Children, do you know what Ephesians 6 says? It admonishes you to obey your parents."

Maria sighs. "This is so stupid."

The DVD starts playing in slow motion and then it skips ahead. Miss Valerie turns the lights on and goes to the DVD player. "I don't know what's wrong with this thing," she says. She takes the disk out and wipes it on her skirt; then she puts it back in.

We start watching the DVD again. This time we get farther. A young boy is told by his parents not to ride his bike past a certain point, but he does it anyway. The little boy is in the middle of the street when a car comes speeding by. The DVD starts skipping forward again.

Miss Valerie turns the lights on. "Okay, what's going on here?" She searches her desk for the remote control and realizes it's not there. "Who has the remote?" Miss Valerie stands with her hands on her hips.

There are small sounds of giggling from behind me and I turn around. A row of boys are laughing and all of them have their hands in awkward places—in their pockets or tucked under their folded arms. I look at Danny, who is sitting in the last row next to a boy named Ricky. Ricky is the same age as Danny, but he is so tall that he looks older than all of us. His shirt is wrinkled and is tucked halfway into his khaki pants. His hair is braided straight back in cornrows and his lips are shining, like he put on too much ChapStick. Danny and Ricky are hiding their hands too. The only difference between them and other boys is they are the only ones not laughing. I know it's them.

"I am very disappointed in you all," Miss Valerie says. She is trying to sound older than she is. She is not a real teacher. She is in college and only graduated from high school last May. She makes us put "Miss" in front of her first name because it shows respect, she says. But I think she just wants to seem important. "Do I have to check everyone's hands?" Miss Valerie starts walking through the rows of metal chairs.

Those of us in the front hold our hands up with all ten fingers stretched wide. By the time she gets to the back I feel Maria tap me on my leg. I look down and she is tapping me with the remote. It has been passed from the back row. I turn around and Miss Valerie is standing in front of Danny and Ricky. Their hands are stretched open for her to see. "Put it on her desk," Maria whispers.

I just look at her. I can't do that. My grandmother could find out.

"Do it!" Maria whispers louder.

"No," I whisper back.

Maria looks over her shoulder. "She won't know it was you," she says. She hands me the remote.

I take it and run on my tippy-toes to Miss Valerie's desk. I put it next to her Bible and rush back to my seat before she turns around. Maria nudges me. "Stop looking so guilty."

Two girls, Karen and Sabrina, are sitting at the end of our row and they can't stop laughing. Soon we are all laughing and I wonder if God thinks this is funny.

Miss Valerie comes to the front of the room and begins to lecture us about playing in the Lord's house. "One of you has the remote and I know it!"

"You mean *that* remote?" Maria says. She points to Miss Valerie's desk.

Miss Valerie looks at the desk, then back at us. "I'm telling your parents," she says.

"It's been there the whole time," Maria says.

Then Deacon Harris walks by ringing the bell and the class cheers because we realize we have wasted the whole hour. We get up from our seats and head for the door.

"Wait a minute," Miss Valerie says. "Someone has to share during the wrap-up session." We all get quiet. We have nothing to share because we didn't do anything. "Didn't think about that, did you?" Miss Valerie almost smiles at the fact that now the same kids who just drove her crazy will be in trouble because they have nothing to share with their parents.

Ricky shouts, "Well, if we don't have anything to share they'll think you aren't a good teacher."

Miss Valerie rolls her eyes and grabs a picture off the wall. "Whose is this?" She shows it to all of us, like kindergarten teachers show picture books as they read.

I raise my hand.

"Good. You are sharing today."

"What do I— What am I supposed to say?"

"Talk about why you drew this picture. What it means to you, which Bible story inspired it. I don't know. Say whatever you want." Miss Valerie hands me the picture and we all leave the class.

During the wrap-up session, when Deacon Harris asks, "Who's sharing from the middle school class?" I realize that I am nervous and that I really don't want to do this. And I think how Danny and Ricky and the rest of the class owe me. Miss Valerie too.

I stand at the front of the congregation and say, "I drew this picture after we had a lesson about heaven because it sounds like a place where I want to go." I hold my picture up and show it to everyone. It's a picture of heaven—streets paved with gold, silver gates. Grandma looks at it and she is smiling and clapping and everyone joins her. I colored the angels brown, like my momma.

HALLOWED BE THY NAME

. . . .

Silly. Making crazy faces in the mirror;
dancing and lip-synching to my favorite songs;
telling knock-knock and Laffy Taffy jokes to
Danny all night long.

Empty. Void, blank, abandoned, hollow,
vacant. A big, deep hole inside me. Can't see
it, but I know it's real. The kind of loneliness
only a mother's love can fill.

Red. The color of embarrassed cheeks, winter
noses. The color of kissed lips, scraped knees.
The color of eyes after they've cried. The
color of the kitchen floor, the day my momma
died.

Excellent. Good at spelling, good at cooking, good at drawing, good at math.
Good at memorizing Bible verses, good at reciting them when I'm lonely or sad.

Neat. "Clothes in hamper not on the floor," "Put things you play with back where they belong," "Every morning make your bed" are some of the things my momma said.

Impatient. I can't sleep the night before Christmas. I take cookies out of the oven before it's even time. I stand over the stove, wanting the water to hurry and boil in its pot. I sit by the phone, wishing it was my daddy calling. But it's not.

Trustworthy. Never telling secrets, always keeping promises. Dependable and reliable, honest and responsible.

Young. Not a little girl anymore, not a woman either. Thirteen years old, afraid of what my future holds.

I am taking my time picking out an outfit for the first day of school. I think I'll wear my new jeans and yellow shirt, but I want to look at all my options. I have them spread across my bed. Danny is mad because he wants me to turn off the light. "It's not that serious," he says.

"If it wasn't that serious you wouldn't have asked Grandpa for those shoes," I say. Danny and Grandpa went shopping for new school clothes. Danny got three pairs of jeans, three pairs of khaki pants, and some dress pants for church. He got shirts, jerseys, and sweaters. He got a new pair of shoes too, but he came home mad because Grandpa couldn't afford the pair of Nikes that he wanted.

"If it's not a big deal, then wear something you had last year," I tell him.

"Just hurry up and turn off the light!"

"That's what I thought." I throw a pair of socks at him. He throws his pillow and then we start laughing. Danny runs to his drawer and grabs a bundle of T-shirts that are still wrapped in their plastic. As he lifts his arm to throw it, I block myself by running into the closet. I accidentally slam the door shut because I've pulled it with too much force. I hear the T-shirts hit the door. That could've been my face.

"What are you two doing up there?" Grandma shouts.

"Nothing!" Danny says.

I start banging on the door. "Danny, let me out. I can't open it from in here."

Danny is laughing. He comes close to the door so I can hear him clearly and sings, "*G-o-o-d n-i-g-h-t.*" I can tell that he's flicked the switch because there's no more light shining under the door.

"Danny, I'm not playing with you. Open the door!"

"Now you can take all the time you need to choose your clothes."

I start banging on the door and stomping on the floor. "Let me out!"

"Serenity, what is going on up there?" Grandma yells.

"Danny locked me in the closet!"

Grandpa starts yelling now. "Danny!" I can hear him coming up the steps. "By the time I get up there, you both better be in bed."

Danny opens the door. I push him hard and run to my bed, pushing my clothes to the floor and jumping under my covers. Grandpa stands at the door. "You two stop all that horsing around, you hear me?"

"Yes, sir," we say.

"Did you say your prayers?"

"Yes, sir," we lie.

"All right, then, good night." Grandpa goes across the hall to his office. When we hear the door close we start giggling.

Danny whispers, "God's gonna get you for lying to Grandpa."

"You lied too."

"But you're older. You're supposed to be my example."

"Remember that the next time I tell you to do

something," I tell him. And we fall asleep telling each other corny knock-knock and Laffy Taffy jokes.

• • • • • • •

Grandpa drives us to school the next morning. "Your grandma will pick you up and take you to your appointment, okay? You guys have your first session today," Grandpa reminds us. When the school found out about what happened to my momma, they offered to pay for me and Danny to talk to a grief counselor. "All right, have a good day. I'll see you tonight."

Once Danny and I are out of the car, we get separated as we walk through the crowd of wet students, who are holding their umbrellas tight and splashing puddles with their rubber boots. Rose City Academy is about the same size as Eagle Creek, but everything is prettier here. The paint looks fresh, the playground has nets on the basketball hoops, and there are teachers standing outside to greet us. The bell rings and I call out to Danny, "Meet me after school!"

"Where?"

I look around trying to find a good meeting place. I point to the flagpole with its red, white, and blue flag dancing in the wind. "There."

"All right," he says and he walks away toward the seventh grade hall.

I take my schedule out of my folder and look for room

306. I have English, my favorite subject, first. After I put my wet coat in my locker, I find my class. "Serenity?" Someone yells my name as I walk into class. "Hey, girl!" It's Maria.

We sit together. "I didn't know you went here," I say. I'm glad I know at least one person in this school.

"Yep, been here since the sixth grade." Maria scoots over so I have room.

"You like it?"

"It's all right. School is school, you know?"

"Yeah." I put my notebook down, face up, on the desk. I have slid a few pictures of my friends from my old school in the plastic sleeve. I have a picture of my momma in my backpack too. I'll always carry it with me, but I don't take it out. I hang my backpack on the back of my chair. Maria looks different today. Her hair is straight, no curls. And she is wearing makeup.

Students start piling in the classroom. Friends sit next to each other and catch up, swapping vacation stories. "What other classes do you have?" I ask Maria.

She shows me her schedule. We have two more classes—health and science—together.

The tardy bell rings and Mrs. Ross, our teacher, begins class. "Once I learn your names, I won't have to take roll this way, but for now, please say here when I say your name." Mrs. Ross reads from a list and checks off names as people respond. She gets through the Ds, then calls out, "Serenity?"

"Here," I say.

"Serenity Evans?" she says, checking her list again, then looking back at me.

"Yes."

She stares at me. "I know you. I mean, well, I knew your mom. I, ah, I went to high school with her." She stops talking and just stares at me. Now the whole class is looking at me. "Ah, welcome—I'm glad you're, ah, it's nice to meet you."

If I was light skinned, my face would be red. My cheeks are hot and I feel my leg shaking under the table. I was wrong about Rose City Academy. Eagle Creek would have been better. I bite my lip. Mrs. Ross finishes roll and I barely listen to anything else she says until I notice her taping three pictures on the board. Under each picture, she tapes their names: Maya Angelou, Sandra Cisneros, Langston Hughes.

"This year we're going to be studying poetry and writing some of our own. Every Friday will be our Poetry Workshop," Mrs. Ross explains. She walks around the room as she talks. "You all must get a journal. Your journal will be for you to practice using the literary devices we learn in class," she says. "You may also use your journal to record some of your favorite lines or quotes from the poems we read." Mrs. Ross walks back to the front of the room. "Your weekly journal entries are different from class assignments. They are for your eyes only. I won't be reading what you write in your journal."

I am real glad when I hear this. The pages in my journal are the keepers of my secrets. I don't want anyone reading them.

Mrs. Ross passes out a worksheet. "These vocabulary words that I am passing out to you are what poets call literary devices. We'll talk about that more in a moment. Right now, let's get started with a free write."

Mrs. Ross tells us that a free write has no rules. We can write about anything we want for five minutes. I write how I already have a journal and how I like to write and how I think I'll do well in this class.

At the end of class, I tell Mrs. Ross about my journal. I don't tell her my daddy gave it to me. I just say, "It already has writing in it from during the summer, but can I use it for your class anyway?"

Mrs. Ross smiles at me. "Sure, Serenity. I think that's a great idea."

"Thanks, Mrs. Ross. See you tomorrow."

Maria and I leave English. I have math next. Maria points me in the right direction. "Look for me at lunch," she says.

"Okay." We hug each other and Maria walks down the hall.

Even though Maria told me which way to go, I get lost. Somehow I've ended up back in front of Mrs. Ross's class. The tardy bell rings and students vanish into their classrooms. Teachers close their doors and I'm left alone standing in the hallway.

Great. I'm going to be late on the first day of school. I stand there and look at the numbers on the classrooms, then at my schedule. I see a guy walking toward me. He looks too tall to be a student, but once he gets closer I can tell he's the same age as me. His hair is neatly braided in cornrows. His baggy jeans fit him perfectly, not sagging too low, not too tight. "Excuse me, do you know where Mr. Nelson's class is?"

"Yeah. Come with me. That's my next class," he says. He doesn't seem to be concerned that he's late. "You new?"

"Yeah. I transferred from Eagle Creek," I tell him.

"You went to the Creek? My boy Greg goes there."

"Greg Roberts?"

"Yeah."

Greg got kicked out of class almost every day last year. Even on the last day of school.

"What's your name?" he asks.

"Serenity."

"I'm Jay," he says. We get to room 407 and he opens the door.

"Thanks for walking me to class."

"You're welcome."

When we step in the class, the teacher gives us an evil eye. "Do either of you have hall passes?"

"I got lost and he—"

"I don't need no pass," Jay says. He turns to the class. "Everybody, this is Serenity. She's from the Creek." He pulls out a chair for me. I sit down. Random people say hi to me.

Jay continues. "I was asked to show her around the school. Sorry we're late."

I think the teacher knows he's lying. But he doesn't care. He checks our names off on his roll sheet and asks a student to pass out the math books. "Turn to page twenty-five," he says.

I open the book to page twenty-five. Jay doesn't open his. He puts his hat on and slouches down in his seat. "No hats in class," Mr. Nelson shouts. "You know the rules." He takes Jay's hat from off his head. "You'll get it back after school. Now come on, you're wasting time." Mr. Nelson goes back to the dry erase board.

"I was paying attention. It's not like I was doing anything," Jay mumbles.

"I don't make the rules," Mr. Nelson says.

Jay leans back in his chair. He mumbles something under his breath about Mr. Nelson, and the students at our table burst into laughter. "All right, Jay. Move," Mr. Nelson says. He points to another table that has no one sitting at it. Jay doesn't move. "Now," Mr. Nelson says.

Jay gets up and sits at the table. Mr. Nelson takes his math book and opens it to page twenty-five. "Let's start the year off right," Mr. Nelson says. When Mr. Nelson turns his back to write on the board, Jay closes his book. He reaches into his pocket and pulls out a stack of bills.

He counts them. The green is moving so fast in his hands, I can't keep up with how much money he has. He must feel me staring at him because he looks across the aisle at me. I try to play it off, like I wasn't just looking at him, like I don't see all that green in his hands. Our eyes meet. I look away.

When the bell rings, Jay asks, "You good, or you need me to take you to your next class?"

"I'm good," I say. I know where my health class is. It's right next to Mrs. Ross's class. But I wouldn't mind it if he walked with me.

"All right, then," Jay says. "See you later."

Before going to health, I stop at the water fountain. The water comes out in slow motion—little squirts—just enough to barely wet my tongue. Mrs. Ross is standing near the fountain with another teacher, Mrs. Wilson. Mrs. Wilson whispers, "You remember Loretta Evans, don't you? That's her child right there." I figure Mrs. Wilson is pointing at me, and I am uncomfortable knowing someone is looking at me while I'm bent over. "You heard about what happened, right?" she asks.

And I think about what Grandma always says about the truth following you wherever you go.

"Yeah. I know. Serenity is in my class," Mrs. Ross says.

Mrs. Wilson sighs. "Terrible thing Loretta put them kids through," she says. "Poor girl. Hope she don't end up like her momma."

"Me too," Mrs. Ross says.

I slurp my last sip and walk away hearing Mrs. Wilson say, "Well, you know what they say—the fruit don't fall far from the tree."

I don't know how it is that Maria knows just when to show up, but here she is walking toward me from down the hall just as my tears fall. "What's the matter?" Maria swings her backpack on her right shoulder.

"Nothing," I say, wiping my eyes. I just keep walking. I want to find a bathroom, but I don't know which way to go.

"Here, come with me." Maria turns right at the end of the hall and two doors down there's a bathroom. Three girls are standing in the mirror fixing their hair and reapplying their lip gloss. Maria takes me into a stall. She locks the door.

"What's the matter?" Maria asks again.

I can't talk. I'm choking on my tears and I can barely breathe.

"Is somebody talking about you? Tell me who it is and I'll go find them right now."

I shake my head no.

"Are you sick?"

I shake my head again.

Maria just looks at me. And it's like we have an entire conversation with our eyes. "You don't have to tell me unless you want to."

I take a few deep breaths.

"All right," Maria says. "Here." She pulls toilet paper out of the dispenser and hands it to me. "Blow your nose and clean your face." Then she says, "Don't wipe too hard—that tissue is so tough it'll cut you."

I smile.

Maria leaves the stall. I hear the girls asking her what's wrong with me. "She's okay," Maria says. "Everything's going to be fine." Maria says it so firmly that I believe her.

I come out of the stall so we are not late for class. The three girls that were in the bathroom are in my health class too. We also see them—Lisa, Denise, and Sommer—in English. They keep looking at us. Maria turns and whispers to me, "Ask them if they got a staring problem!"

I tell Maria that I am fine. I take my notebook out and start to write my name over and over in different styles—bubble letters, cursive, print. Then out of nowhere, Maria grabs my notebook and tears out the sheet of paper I am writing on.

"You want her autograph or something?" She throws the paper at them. "Serenity, I didn't know you were a celebrity. Girl, I'm high status hanging around you." Some of the class laughs. Lisa, Denise, and Sommer don't. They roll their eyes. Lisa takes the paper, balls it up, and throws it away. When she walks past Maria, I think they might fight, but Lisa goes back to her seat, not saying a word. I think Maria could take her down. Which is probably why Lisa just sits back in her seat. Lisa looks like the type of girl who'd call an older sister or cousin to fight for her. Maria doesn't need anyone but herself. They are both pretty and I think maybe that is why they don't like each other. Denise and Sommer, Lisa's shadows, are pretty too, but they are more regular. Kind of like me.

"I can't stand those girls," Maria says.

I turn and look at Maria's enemies. They are dressed in outfits that look like they've come straight off a mannequin. When Lisa finally talks later in class, she says, "Like, oh my God!" a million times and all three of them laugh and toss their hair over their shoulders every five seconds. If I closed my eyes, I would think they were on some reality show about cheerleaders.

Mr. Harvey finishes taking roll and tells us about all the things we will learn this school year. When he mentions sex and sexually transmitted diseases a few students start laughing.

At the end of school, I get my coat from my locker and meet Danny at the flagpole. He is standing there with Ricky. "Hi, Ricky. You go here too?" Ricky looks more our age now that he is dressed in jeans. His pants are sagging and so are Danny's.

"That's a stupid question," Danny says. "If he didn't go here, would he be standing here right now?"

I hit Danny in his chest.

"God, Ricky," Maria says. "We're going to school with

the pastor's grandchildren. They're going to tell him every bad thing we do."

"Or," Ricky says, "we'll just have to get them to do bad stuff with us so we can blackmail them."

We laugh.

I see Grandma's car pull up behind the line of other parents waiting for their children. "Come on, Danny. We gotta go." We all say good-bye to each other. Danny pulls his jeans up on our way to the car.

The closer we get to the counseling office, the less we talk. At first Danny and I are telling Grandma about our day—I only tell the good things, how Maria is in three of my classes and how I've already remembered my locker combination. Danny tells Grandma about his favorite classes, math and gym. But when we pull in the parking lot of Providence Children's Center, we both stop talking.

• • • • • • •

"I'll be out here in the waiting room," Grandma says to us as two women take me and Danny in separate rooms.

Danny walks away with a woman named Gloria. She is short and fat and she has on three shades of blue. Her brown curly hair falls in her face and she talks like she's asking a question. "Right this way," she tells Danny, her voice raised at the end of the sentence as if Danny has a choice.

I go with Ann. She has on a long gray skirt and a dark burgundy blouse. When we go in her office, she smiles at me, points to the sofa, and sits across from me in an armchair.

The first thing she says to me is, "Serenity. What a beautiful name." She crosses her legs. I notice her nylons twisting around her ankles. "Do you know what your name means?"

"People tell me it means 'peace,'" I tell Ann. "But I don't think names mean anything. They are just what you are called so people can get your attention or yell at you."

Ann shifts in her seat. "Do you feel peace, Serenity?"

"The preachers at church say we'll have peace when we get to heaven," I say.

Ann asks, "Do you want peace now—here on earth?"

I nod my head. "I don't understand why we have to wait."

Ann clears her throat. "You started school today, right?"

"Yeah."

"How was it?"

"Fine," I answer.

"What was the best part?"

"Um, well, I guess having my friend Maria from church there," I say.

"That's nice. To have someone you know there."

"Yeah. Maria is nice."

"What are some of the things you like about her?" Ann talks slow and soft. I can barely hear her sometimes because of the heavy rain that is hitting the window. I watch the drops of water race each other, then disappear once they hit the windowpane. "Serenity—what do you like about Maria?"

I say the first thing that comes to mind. "She doesn't make me talk when I don't want to."

Ann takes a sip of her coffee. "You don't want to talk?"

"I don't know what to say."

"You're doing fine," Ann says. "There's not something you *have* to say." She pauses and smiles at me. "And you know, you can talk to me about anything. Nothing has to be off-limits." Ann closes her notebook. "Can you tell me what the worst thing was that happened today?"

I didn't know I still had tears left over from earlier. They come out before any words do. I can't believe I've started crying so easily. Twice in one day. I finally catch my breath and say, "I don't like Mrs. Wilson."

"Who is Mrs. Wilson?"

"A teacher at my school. Her classroom is right next to my English class."

"Why don't you like her?" Ann asks.

"She thinks I'm going to end up like my momma."

"What do you think?"

More tears.

"What do you think you'd be like if you ended up like your mother?"

"I'd marry the wrong guy and make excuses for him," I say.

Ann asks, "How else would you be?"

I feel hot.

Ann asks again.

I tell her, "I'd always be hiding bruises."

"Your father was abusive?"

I really don't want to tell my momma's secrets. I look down at the floor. The tears falling make my eyes blurry and the carpet looks like it's moving. I can barely get the word out. "Yes," I say. "He beat her all the time for no reason at all." Part of our secret is out. It hovers in the room like a heavy rain cloud. "I don't want to live like that," I tell Ann.

"Do you think you have a choice?" Ann asks.

I shrug my shoulders, then shake my head. Now I can't stop crying.

THY KINGDOM COME

· · · · · · · · · ·

Serenity Evans
Mrs. Ross, 1st Period
Poetry Workshop

> **Simile:** *Comparing two unlikely things
> using* like *or* as*: The snow covered the ground
> like a thick blanket. Write a poem about your
> family using similes.*

My Family

My family is like a roller coaster
going up and down, high and low
through the joys and pains of life.

My father's anger was like hot, boiling water.
My mother's tears
fell down her cheeks like waterfalls.
My brother hid like a turtle
disappearing in its shell.
My grandparents' house
is like a shelter for stray puppies.

My family is like a roller coaster
going up and down, high and low
through the joys and pains of life.

The weekend is full of the usual. Friday night I go with
Danny, Ricky, and Maria to the youth group's bowling
party. Saturday I go grocery shopping with Grandma for
the soup kitchen and Sunday we go to church.

Grandpa is still taking a break from preaching, but
he and Grandma stay busy with the church and I think
that helps them keep their minds off my momma, because
whenever they stand still, even for a moment, they break
into sobs. They still don't know I can hear them through
the vents. Whenever they're sad, they go into their room
and cry.

Last week I accidentally walked in on Grandma
while she was looking through old photo albums and
crying. She was sitting on her bed looking at a picture of
my momma when she was a baby. I sat next to her and

she flipped through the pages telling me all kinds of stories—Momma's first word, her favorite toy, the day she graduated from high school. There is such sadness in Grandma's eyes. And I never thought about it till that moment, but I bet it hurts just as bad to lose a daughter as it does to lose a mother.

Danny doesn't cry as much. Grandpa says everyone experiences grief in different ways. Danny's way is not doing his homework, sneaking out of church, and talking back. He's been in trouble at school twice this week for getting smart with a teacher. Grandma has a teacher conference because of it next Friday.

When we go to church, you'd never know we were so messed up and sad at home. Like today. Grandma is singing in the choir, raising her hands to God in praise. And Grandpa is sitting in the pulpit, smiling and nodding his head in agreement with what the preacher is saying.

There is a guest minister today. He is the pastor at New Joy Tabernacle. His name is Pastor McGee. He is fat like Santa Claus but he doesn't have a beard, and his suit is navy blue. He's been to the house for dinner, always wearing dark suits. He never wears bright colors like his wife, who is known for her fluorescent dresses and gigantic matching hats. Every time she visits our church she sits in the third row. I'm sure anyone who sits behind her can't see the pulpit. Mrs. McGee fans herself with the bulletin, yelling piercing cheers, rooting for her husband. "Preach, Pastor! I know that's right. Tell it like it is. Amen!"

Pastor McGee tells us to turn our Bibles to John 15. I open the Bible Grandma gave me but can't find where John is, so I pretend that I have to get something out of my purse. Maria sees me. She scoots close to me and we read her Bible together. We follow along with Pastor McGee as he reads aloud. Maria's finger slides across the thin paper guiding my eyes. "Jesus' words are in red," she whispers.

While we are reading, Karen passes a folded square to Maria. Maria opens it and we read the letter, only it looks like we are still reading the scripture. The letter is from Ricky, who is sitting behind us. I turn around. Ricky looks cute today. He always does, but Maria doesn't think so. Ricky is too simple for her. Maria is a fancy girl. Her lips are always glossed and smell like strawberries. She matches everything—her shoes with her bag, her socks with her shirts. And her eyes are a light hazel brown, but not really. One day in the bathroom at school, she took out her contacts because they were irritating her eyes. Her eyes are dark brown like mine.

I am looking at the note, with its crease in the middle of the sentence. Ricky wants to know if she will go with him. Maria writes back, "Go where?" And we laugh out loud. Grandma gives me a look from the choir stand and I know when I get home I will get a lecture about respecting God's house.

Communion is passed and in unison we drink small cups of grape juice, smaller than the cup that comes with cough medicine. We eat the crisp, flat wafer, and Pastor McGee reads a scripture about Jesus dying on the cross and rising on the third day. Maria accidentally drops her cup of grape juice, and Mrs. McGee turns around and clears her throat. She doesn't like us. She is always clearing her throat and glaring at us from under her too-big hats. She is the only adult at church who never offers us any peppermint candies.

I do not pay attention to where Danny is until Grandpa asks me when church is over. I go outside to find him. "Ricky, have you seen Danny?"

"Nope. Not since Sunday school." That was over an hour ago.

As I walk down the steps of the church, I see Danny walking up the sidewalk. He is with Jay. This is the third time Danny has left church to be with Jay. Jay smiles at me. "What's up?" He tosses his head up in the air and asks, "You good?" Ever since the first day of school, he asks me this whenever he sees me.

"I'm good," I tell him. I wonder what he'd do if I said I wasn't. "Danny, Grandpa is looking for you."

"I'm right here," he says. Danny's eyes are light pink and they sit low. "You got some eye drops, Maria?"

"I think so. Let me see." Maria looks in her purse, pulls out a small bottle, and gives it to Danny.

"Thanks." Danny squirts the last drop right when

Grandma comes outside. She doesn't ask any questions and we don't say anything. We just wait for Grandpa to bring the car around. Grandma taps her foot against the cement, humming the song she sang today in the choir. Grandma always hums when she is angry. I think my lecture won't be too long. Grandma is more upset with Danny.

On the ride home everyone is silent. Except Grandma. She is still humming. When Grandpa pulls the car into the driveway, we get out and go into the house. Danny tosses his Bible on the floor in the living room and starts setting up his video game.

"Boy, have you lost your mind? Pick that Bible up off the floor and put that game away!" Grandma is standing with her hand on her hip.

"But, Grandma—" Danny is whining.

"Don't talk back to me. Go to your room. Don't come out till I call you."

Danny huffs and puffs and loudly sucks his teeth, but does what Grandma says.

Grandma gives him her stern look. "Something caught in your teeth?"

"No, Grandma." Danny goes to our room. I follow him. "Don't start with me," he says. He takes his shoes off, but not the rest of his clothes, and stretches out across his bed.

"What do you mean don't start? You started it by

leaving church. Why are you giving Grandma a reason to fuss at you?"

"I ain't giving her or you no reason to say nothin' to me!"

"You left church!" I say. Then I lower my voice. "And you're smoking weed. Are you crazy?"

Danny gets up and goes into the bathroom, even though I can tell he doesn't have to use it. He just doesn't have any other place to go. I stand at the door trying to think of something to say to him, but I can't think of anything that won't make him more mad. So I just go in my room and change out of my church clothes.

I try to start my homework, but all I'm doing is doodling and drawing on my paper. I've been wasting time for about an hour when my grandma lets us know it's time for dinner.

"All right, you two, time to eat!" Grandma calls us and we go to the dining room. Grandpa says a prayer over the food and we all start eating. "Honey, you've outdone yourself," he says as he eats Grandma's rice and gravy. "You need to go ahead and write that cookbook you keep talking about." Grandpa scrapes the last bit of food off his plate. Grandma just smiles and serves him another helping. "Serenity, did you know your grandma is going to put a cookbook together?"

"No," I say. I eat a bite of my pork chop.

"We'll sell it locally first, but I know it will be a

success. People are always asking your grandmother for recipes. Isn't that right, sweetie?"

Grandma nods her head. "I know hundreds of recipes. Serenity, I was hoping you'd help me make some of them, test them out, and see which ones should go in the book. Would you like to help?"

"I have too much homework," I tell her. Now I just want to get up and leave the table. I do not want to talk about cooking. I have lost my appetite and take a drink of my water.

Grandpa looks at Danny. "Bet you could make time for taste testing, huh?"

Danny shrugs his shoulders but half smiles, happy that someone has finally talked to him. I think he feels less in trouble now that he's a part of the conversation.

Grandma clears her throat. "Mr. Daniel Lee Evans won't be doing any special activities if he skips out on church again." She looks at him, one eyebrow arched, her lips pursed together. "I don't like that Jay boy. You don't need to be hanging around him."

"You don't even know him," Danny says, avoiding her eyes. "Why don't you like him?"

"I think you know the answer to that question, Danny." Grandma looks at my grandpa like she wants him to say something.

Grandpa says, "He's not a bad person. He's just not doing anything positive. We don't want you picking up his ways. I hear Jay barely goes to school," Grandpa says.

"It's like the Bible says, 'Bad company ruins good intentions.'"

Danny looks at Grandpa and asks, half defiant and half sincere, "Where does it say that?"

"First Corinthians 15:33," I blurt out. Then I feel bad for making it seem like I'm a know-it-all. I only know because it was a memory verse last week. I want to tell Danny that I don't know everything, that I couldn't even find the verse in church today. But I don't say anything.

Grandma asks if we have finished our homework. We both say no. Danny says he has to finish his math. "What do you have left?" Grandma asks me.

"I have to read one of Maya Angelou's poems and write a reflection." Grandma asks me which one. I excuse myself from the table and get my folder. I pull out the handout Mrs. Ross gave us. "'Still I Rise,'" I tell her.

Grandpa sits back in his chair, looking too full to eat another bite. "That's one of your favorites, isn't it?" he says to Grandma.

"Yes, indeed. I love that poem. Seems like Maya wrote that one about me." Grandma recites part of her favorite stanza. She performs the poem like she's on stage, softening her voice or making it loud for dramatic effect. Then Grandma shouts the last line, lifting her hands to the ceiling. She smiles. "Yes, indeed, I've risen out of many, many things. That poem was written for me." She starts to clear the table.

Grandpa chuckles. "I'm sure everyone feels that way."

Grandma opens the dishwasher and begins loading it. "I suppose you're right," she says. "Everybody's risen out of something, huh?"

"What have you risen out of, Grandma?" I ask.

"Lots of things." Grandma stops loading the dishwasher and leans against the kitchen counter.

Grandpa reminds us, "You children have heard the stories of how we marched and protested for our very freedom. For rights and equality." He tells us stories about how it was growing up in the South when he was our age.

"But we rose out of segregation!" Grandma yells. "And we've overcome some personal battles."

Grandpa adds, "Your aunt Sara was a very sick child. There were many times we thought she wasn't going to make it."

"And we rose out of sickness!" Grandma shouts.

"And Lord knows, we've had our share of times counting pennies, making ends meet."

Grandma's voice gets even louder. "And we rose out of poverty!"

Danny and I laugh. He isn't mad anymore and we're all sitting around the dining room table talking about all the good things that have happened in our family. Grandma and Grandpa go on and on for a while. They tell us about how their church used to be a tiny storefront. Less than twenty members and now it's grown to be one of the largest churches in Portland.

"That's why we say 'we rise,' children. There have been lots of things that have tried to keep us down. But we've got resilience running through these veins. And so do the both you," she says.

Grandma gets back to cleaning the kitchen. She wipes the counter with a dishrag. Grandpa puts his arm around her waist, takes the rag, and says, "Go sit down, honey. You've worked hard enough today." Grandpa finishes cleaning. "Danny, take out the trash, please," he says as he starts the dishwasher.

Danny ties the black plastic bag in a knot and pulls it out of the can. He takes it outside and when he comes back to the kitchen, he puts a new bag in the trash can.

I have never seen a man do house chores before. The only time I saw my daddy in the kitchen was when he was getting a beer out of the fridge. I always helped my momma wash the dishes and clean up after dinner. Sitting here in the kitchen makes me think of her.

Memories of my momma pop in my head at the most unexpected times. Like when I sing the lyrics to a song I didn't even realize I knew. Momma is a song I can't forget. Her melody comes to mind and I realize that traces of her song are still here.

When I helped Momma clean the kitchen, she would tell me her plans for the future. "One day, Serenity, I'm gonna own my own restaurant and I'm gonna have a whole crew of people for the dishes."

"Will you have people who'll set the tables too?"

"Yep. I'm gonna have all of that. All I'm gonna do is be the chef and one day some food critic from the *Oregonian* will come and ask if he can speak with the chef, and I'll come out and he'll tell me how wonderful the meal is."

"And he'll write about you in the paper and everyone in Portland will come," I added.

"That's right," Momma said. We had rehearsed the story a thousand times. But every time we said it, it seemed like the first. I hate that my mom made it to the paper for a different reason.

I help Grandpa load the dishwasher, and when we are finished I go into the living room with Grandma and Danny. I sit next to Grandma and for some reason, I want to lie on her, snuggle up against her like she's a pillow, like when I was little. She runs her fingers through my hair and says, "You and Maria need to stop giggling and carrying on in church, okay?"

"Okay," I say. Danny looks at me, and I know he is happy that I got fussed at too, even if it wasn't that bad.

As we watch TV, the doorbell rings. Grandma gets up, breathing heavy, and walks toward the door. "You expecting company?" she says to Grandpa, who is dozing off in his armchair.

I think that maybe it's my daddy. Maybe he's come back from wherever he was and he knew where to find us. I don't think about him as much as I used to. Danny has taken the calendar down in our room. Sometimes hope hurts too bad to hold on to it, so I think part of me has stopped believing that he'll come back. And if he does, I'd rather be surprised than to keep waiting for something and be disappointed.

Grandma opens the door. "Well, well, look at this!" She wraps her arms around Erica, my cousin, and her mother, Aunt Sara. Aunt Sara is my grandma's oldest. Erica is her only child. She is twenty-five years old. She has hair that hangs past her shoulders, stopping at the middle of her back. Her dark brown skin looks good in any color, especially bright ones. Like the deep fuchsia V-neck sweater she is wearing today with her dark jeans.

Erica steps inside, hugs Grandpa and Grandma first, then me, then Danny. "How are you?" she says to all of us.

"Good," we answer.

Erica smiles. "Well, Grandma, Grandpa—Mom and I have an announcement to make."

Aunt Sara laughs. "*You* have an announcement to make," she says.

Grandma looks impatient. She is turning her head side to side like people do at tennis matches, looking at Aunt Sara, then at Erica. "What's the news? What's going on?"

"Well," Erica says. "Ivan asked me to be his wife today, and I said yes!" Erica is glowing brighter than the platinum ring on her finger. "Isn't it beautiful?"

"Absolutely lovely!" Grandma hugs Erica. "Congratulations. I am so happy for you. Oh, James—isn't this wonderful?"

Grandpa is smiling. "Yes, it is. It really is. That Ivan, he's a good man."

Grandma shakes her head in disbelief. "I can't believe you all are so grown now. I remember teaching Ivan when he was in the sixth grade. Who would have thought I was teaching a future family member." Grandma laughs. Then she says, "I suppose you'll want me to cater?"

"Of course," Erica says. "And I want Grandpa to do the ceremony."

Grandpa chuckles. "You've got this all figured out, huh? Didn't the boy just propose today?"

We are all laughing. "Grandpa, I've had my wedding planned since I was Serenity's age," she says. "Simple, but elegant white dress. No more than five bridesmaids. Lavender, silver, and white will be the colors."

"Does Ivan have any say?" Grandpa asks.

"Not really," Erica says.

Grandpa shakes his head. "You hear this, Danny? All us men get to do is show up." Grandpa stands. "Come on, son, let's get out of here so the ladies can plan." Before he leaves the living room, he kisses Erica on her forehead. "Congratulations. Let me know if you need anything." Grandpa and Danny go to the garage to work on his car.

Aunt Sara and Grandma go into the kitchen and start writing out a guest list. Erica pulls out a bridal magazine from her black leather tote bag. "Want to help me look for a dress?"

I scoot close to her so I can see the pictures. "I can't believe you're getting married!"

"I know. I'm so excited." Erica flips through the glossy advertisement pages at the front of the magazine and stops once she gets to a dress. "You want to get married one day?"

I shrug my shoulders.

"You have a boyfriend?"

"No!" I yell. "Grandma is not having that."

"Do you like anyone at school?"

"No."

"At church?"

"No."

"Why not?"

"I don't know," I tell Erica. I point to a dress that looks like something Erica would like. It's strapless and is tight around the waist but then puffs out into a big skirt. "That's cute," I say.

"Yeah, I like it," Erica says, "but don't try to change the subject." She folds the right corner of the page and turns to the next picture. "You don't have a crush on *anyone*?"

"No, I swear."

"There are no cute boys at school?"

"Well, not really. I mean—well, there's one. But he's—"

"He's what?"

"He's bad," I tell Erica.

"Like what kind of bad?"

I lower my voice. "He smokes weed and I think he sells it too. He's always skipping school, and today Danny got in trouble for leaving church to be with him."

"What's his name?"

"Jay," I whisper. "But, Erica, he is so cute."

"The bad ones always are," Erica tells me. "But don't let those good looks get you caught up." She turns down another corner of the magazine.

"I won't," I tell Erica.

Erica takes out a different magazine. This one is of bridesmaid's dresses. "And look out for Danny. Sounds like he shouldn't be hanging around him either."

"Danny thinks I'm bossy. He doesn't listen to me."

"Believe me, girl, Danny hears you. It may not seem like he's listening, but he is. So keep talking to him. You two need each other. There's nothing more important than family," Erica says.

We look through a few more magazines and then Erica sets them aside. "I have something important to ask you," she says.

I get a lump in my throat. Please don't ask me how I'm doing, or have the nightmares stopped, or am I ready to talk about it.

Erica smiles. "I wanted to know if you would like to be my junior bridesmaid."

"For real?" I say.

Erica nods. "I'd love for you to be in the wedding."

"Of course!" I yell. "I can't wait to tell Maria," I say.

"Who's Maria?" Erica asks.

"My friend," I say. "I met her at church and we go to the same school."

"That's great," Erica says. "I'm glad you have a friend you can talk to."

Here it comes.

"It's important to talk to people, Serenity. To let it out," Erica says.

"I'm in counseling," I tell her.

"I know," she says. "But talking with family and friends is important too."

I open one of the magazines and flip through the pages. "I don't have anything to say," I tell Erica.

"Well, I'm here for you when you do."

I start feeling real bad for what I told Maria. The lie about my momma being in a car accident was so easy to tell. My momma lied a lot. To my grandma, to neighbors, to me.

Grandma would ask about her bruises. My momma would lie and say she fell.

Neighbors would ask about the noise. My momma would lie and say no one was fighting.

I'd ask her if she was okay. My momma would lie and say she was.

I tell Erica, "Maria asked about my momma and daddy."

"What did you say?"

"I didn't tell the truth," I admit.

"Well, Serenity, the truth is always better than a lie. No matter how painful it is to tell," Erica says.

For the rest of the night, Erica and I sit on the sofa talking about her and Ivan. She tells me about the honeymoon they're going on, the house they're going to move into, and the kids they're going to have. She wants two.

I am excited about Erica's wedding. It will be nice to have the whole family together for something good. The last time we all gathered, it was for my momma's funeral.

THY WILL BE DONE, IN EARTH

· · · · · · · · · · ·

Serenity Evans
Mrs. Ross, 1st Period
Poetry Workshop

> **Alliteration:** *Words that begin with the same sounds: Peter Piper picked a peck of pickled peppers.*
>
> *What do you wish for?*
> *Write a poem about it using alliteration.*

To be with my momma
making marvelous miracles
in the kitchen again.

To stop seeing Danny sink steadily.
To be beautiful, bold, and brave.
I wish wishing would work.

It's been raining on and off for two weeks. Sometimes it's an on-and-off drizzle, sometimes sprinkles; today it's storming. The sky is gray and it gets dark earlier now. October is the worst time of year to go on a weekend youth retreat. We can barely do any of the outdoor activities in Bend because everything is soggy and wet. Five hours of riding on this charter bus and we can't even go horseback riding or white-water rafting like the brochure said.

"Whoever planned this trip needs to be fired," Maria says to me. The bus is making us bounce up and down. Her cheeks vibrate. "You need to start using that PK power you have and tell your grandfather what's going on."

I just shake my head at Maria. I keep telling her that just because I'm the pastor's granddaughter doesn't mean I can work magic and get my way. "You need to stop talking so loud before you get in trouble again," I tell her. We are sitting two seats behind Miss Valerie and she's had it in for Maria ever since she caught Maria and Ricky kissing behind the baptism pool. Miss Valerie told everybody. Grandma says Maria is too fast for her own good.

Maria and Ricky are boyfriend and girlfriend now. She thinks he is cuter now that she knows him. I think he won her over when he freestyled a rap dedicated to her. That, and he cut his hair, so now it's low and wavy. Maria and Ricky weren't going to be allowed to go on the youth retreat, but Maria wrote an apology letter to my grandpa and Miss Valerie. Ricky did too. I am glad they are here. Maria has become my best friend; sometimes we tell people at school that we are cousins.

Grandpa said this youth retreat is going to be great. Our youth pastor, Pastor Mitchell, and his wife, took a team of kids from our youth group with him to evangelize the streets and invite kids in the neighborhood to come. "That's what the church should do. Be where the people really are," Grandpa said. "He's doing things right."

Pastor Mitchell is definitely doing something. He got Jay to come to the retreat. Everyone thinks that's a miracle. Well, most of us. Some people say that Jay is only coming because of the cute girls, but I figure he sees cute girls every day, so why would he spend a whole weekend in the woods? Jay is sitting with Ricky and Danny at the back of the bus. They are right behind Karen and Sabrina. Karen and Sabrina also go to Rose City Academy. I am just now getting to know them. They are seen with each other so much and act just alike that people say their names like it's one whole word: KarenandSabrina.

"Everyone, listen up!" Miss Valerie is standing at the front of the bus, holding on to the seat so she doesn't fall. "We are about ten minutes away from the cabins. Make sure you clean up all the trash around you and take everything off the bus." She pauses as people move and start doing as she says.

"Listen up, listen up!" Miss Valerie continues. "When we pull into the parking lot, I want you all to exit the bus quietly and go to your assigned cabins. Put your bags in your room and report to the dining hall for dinner," she says. "Please be mindful of the rules," Miss Valerie adds. Then she reads us a list:

1. *No boys are allowed in girls' rooms.*
2. *No girls are allowed in boys' rooms.*
3. *No one can be in the common area or game room past ten p.m.*
4. *No skipping sessions—everyone must attend morning devotion, afternoon Bible study, and evening prayer.*
5. *No disrespect.*
6. *No secular music.*
7. *No television.*
8. *No cell phone usage. If you need to call your parents, you must use the staff phone.*
9. *No wandering off campgrounds without an adult.*
10. *Have fun.*

"Have fun? Well, we would if we didn't have rules one through nine," Ricky shouts.

We all laugh.

"All right, all right." Miss Valerie lifts her arms and lowers them several times like she can control our volume with hand gestures.

The bus pulls into the campgrounds and there are two cabins waiting for us behind a family of trees. The cabin on the left is for the boys, the one on the right is for us girls. There are ten rooms in each cabin. Each cabin has two suites for staff. Maria and I are together. We go straight to our room to drop off our bags and then join everyone for dinner.

When we enter the dining hall, we see Jay, Ricky, and Danny sitting with Karen and Sabrina. We join them. Jay scoots over and makes room for me to sit next to him. Every time I am near him my hands get sweaty. I wipe them on my jeans and try to act like it's no big deal I'm sitting next to the finest boy at the camp.

The kitchen crew serves us macaroni and cheese that's too gooey and thick to swallow. The salad is wilted and the chicken is dry. Maria whispers, "They should have asked your grandma to cook." We drink lots of lemonade and eat the rolls to get full and then have dessert. Vanilla ice cream with chocolate syrup. No one can mess that up.

We have evening Bible study as a group. Pastor Mitchell and his wife welcome us and remind us of the rules. They introduce the leaders that will be helping out. Ivan and Erica are here as extra staff.

Pastor Mitchell dismisses us and tells us we have two hours of free time and then we have to return to our cabins. "Morning prayer and Bible study are at eight o'clock in the morning."

We moan.

Maria and I walk with Karen and Sabrina to explore the campgrounds. The rec room is at the end of a spiraling path, next to the fellowship hall. It has a pool table, air hockey table, and lots of board games. There are also puzzles and books to read. Most of the boys are playing air hockey or pool. We sit with Karen and Sabrina and play Monopoly until it's time to go to our room.

When Maria and I go back to our room, we change into our nightclothes.

"You should let me style your hair," Maria says.

"It's in braids. It is styled."

"Yeah, but you could still do things with it. Like wear it up or something." Maria lifts my braids, bunching them in her hands and holding them up like she's put them into a ponytail. "Let me show you some styles," she says. She goes into her suitcase and gets out hairpins, bobby pins, and two headbands. "Okay, let's start with a bun." She starts styling my hair.

"Who taught you how to do hair?" I ask.

"My mom."

"My mom always did my hair for me. I never really learned how to style it myself," I tell Maria.

"Why don't you ever talk about your mom?" Maria

asks. She sits on the chair at her desk, turning around to face me.

"I don't know, I just, I don't know."

"Tell me about her," Maria says. She tightens the ponytail, then starts pinning the braids all sorts of ways with bobby pins.

"She . . . she could cook just as good as my grandma, she was beautiful, and she loved to laugh."

"Was she driving when she got in the accident?" Maria asks.

I don't say anything.

"Sorry, I should stop trying to make you talk about her."

"It's okay. I want you to know about her. It's just, sometimes when I try to talk about her with you, the words get stuck and I can't say anything."

Maria stops doing my hair. She walks around the chair and sits on the floor in front of me. She takes my hand and doesn't let go. She squeezes tight and it's like she pushes out the pain. I feel hot and nervous and scared. Like I did that day, but that day I didn't say anything. I kept my mouth shut and hid in the closet. But tonight my mouth opens.

"I lied to you." The words come out as a whisper. "My father killed my mother," I confess. "My father killed my mother," I say again. "I've never said these words before." The words feel strange on my tongue, like when I try to speak the Spanish words Maria teaches me. "I keep telling myself that he didn't mean to. That he didn't realize what he had done. But now? Now I'm not sure."

Maria doesn't move. I keep talking.

"My parents always fought. My dad beat my mom all the time. And after a fight, he always stormed out of the house, to give my mom time to clear her head and so he could go cool down," I explain. "Most times, he came back in a few days with flowers or jewelry for her and even something for me and Danny. But this time was different. This time was so different."

The words get stuck again and Maria rubs my hand.

"Danny and I were in our hiding place. The closet in the hallway."

I tell Maria how we always hid in the closet when our parents fought. It was a small closet. Just big enough for the two of us and the vacuum cleaner. Nothing hanging. Just a few shelves with paper towels, toilet paper, and cleaning supplies. We stood in the closet, holding hands, listening to the sounds of two pairs of feet walking back and forth. In and out of the kitchen.

"I'm leaving you," my momma had said. "The kids are coming with me." Her black high heels walked away. My father's feet went after her—brand-new white Nikes. I could hear my mother's heels running from my father's angry voice. "I'm tired, Daniel. Tired of living this way. Tired of worrying if you'll get caught. Tired of being ashamed of you—of us." Her feet stomped back to the kitchen. "The kids' clothes—drug money. Our groceries—drug money. This ain't no way to raise a family!"

My father was cursing and yelling louder than I'd ever heard him. "I don't hear you complainin' when I'm givin' you money to get your hair or your nails done. You ain't hollerin' none of this when you buyin' clothes."

"I don't need dirty money. I don't want it anymore," Momma said.

A loud, long beep sounded in the kitchen. The oven's timer went off. My momma's red velvet cake. Momma had prepared a feast. The ham had just been taken out of the oven. The greens were still simmering on the stovetop. She was saving the mashed potatoes for last because they take the least time to cook. I had helped my momma cut and peel the potatoes. They were soaking in water. The garlic cloves were wrapped in foil, just out of the oven. Momma put garlic in her mashed potatoes. She said she learned it from watching my grandma. The house smelled like Thanksgiving even though it was August, and I couldn't wait to eat. But now Momma's dinner was ruined.

The timer continued to beep. Momma's feet ran to the kitchen. The beeping stopped and I heard the oven open and close.

"Is that all you care about? Your stupid cooking?"

"It's not stupid. You are!"

Slap.

My momma was crying now. No more feet walking

back and forth. Just the sound of hands hitting face. And then there were no more slapping sounds. Now my daddy was cursing and choking my momma. He kept asking her why she provoked him. Why she made him be so mean. I could hear her gasping for air and then a thud as my daddy pushed her to the floor.

After that, I heard my daddy's feet running away, out of the kitchen through the side door that led to the driveway. My daddy slammed the door so hard, the house shook.

Maria squeezes my hand tighter.

"When I opened the closet door, I ran to my momma and kneeled down beside her. I expected to help her up and nurse her bruises like I always did. But this time she didn't get up. She was barely breathing and blood was streaming out the side of her head. Her head had hit the edge of the marble kitchen island.

"Danny ran to get the phone and call for an ambulance. I held my mother's hand and told her we had called for help. But then her eyes froze and I knew she was gone.

"Danny and I sat in the kitchen, next to my momma's body. I didn't know what to do. I looked up and saw the prayer over the stove and just kept reading it over and over until the ambulance came."

I can't say anymore. I sit back in the chair. My hand slides out of Maria's.

"I'm so sorry, Serenity." She hugs me. Tight. When

she lets go, I feel lighter. And the knot that's been inside me has untangled a little.

"I'm sorry for lying to you," I tell Maria.

"I understand." Maria crosses her legs. "Is your dad in jail?"

"I don't know where he is," I tell her. "I used to think he didn't know about my momma. I thought he was going to show up to the house with flowers and we'd be gone and he'd come looking for us to tell us how sorry he was. But he hasn't come at all. Never called to check on us. Not even his mom has heard from him," I tell Maria.

"Where do you think he is?" Maria asks.

"I don't know," I answer. "Hiding from the police, I guess."

"You must hate him."

"Part of me does," I tell her. "Part of me wants him to go to jail forever. Sometimes I wish he was the one who died," I admit. "But sometimes—sometimes I get sad and I want him to come back and apologize. I want him to want me and Danny to come stay with him."

"Would you go?"

"No!" I tell Maria. "I would kick and scream and fight to stay with my grandparents," I say. "But at least I'd know he wanted me. At least I'd know he cared," I say. "I know that makes no sense."

"Yes, it does." Maria's eyes are filled with water, but the tears don't fall. Sometimes I wonder what secrets she carries.

It's quiet. The others must be asleep in their rooms. I look out of the window. The sky is black. The white moon shines bright like a lightbulb.

Maria asks, "You have any pictures of your mom?"

I stand up and go to my bag. I pull out the picture I have of my momma. Most of the photographs of her were taken in a studio and she is posing and smiling into the camera because that is what she was supposed to do. Her face is painted in makeup and every strand of her hair is in place. But in this picture, she isn't wearing makeup. She is sitting on the steps of our front porch in a pale yellow sundress. Her wavy hair is blowing in the wind and she isn't looking at the camera. The smile on her face is because she's watching me ride my bike without training wheels for the first time. Danny is behind me, learning too.

My momma is smiling wide. All of her looks happy. And that is why I like this shot so much. It shows me how much my momma loved me. The smile on her face, the joy in her eyes is all because of me. And Danny. And it is real. I know because Grandma took this picture when my momma wasn't expecting it.

Maria reaches out for the picture. She stares at it and looks back up at me. "You're right. She was beautiful. You look just like her."

I smile. Maria thinks I'm pretty. Grandma always says it, but for some reason I believe it more now.

Maria does two more styles on me and tries to show me how to do them too. "Now you have some options other than a ponytail and wearing them down," she says. Maria turns me around to face her. "Okay, now let's do some makeup." She gets a small bag out of her suitcase. "How come you never wear makeup?"

"My grandma would have three heart attacks and a stroke if she saw me in makeup."

Maria laughs at me. "You always do what your grandmother tells you to do?"

"Not always, but—well, I try."

"Goodness, girl, if you don't make it to heaven no one will."

"You can teach me, though. I mean putting on makeup is something I'll need to know how to do once she decides I can wear it."

"Right," Maria says. She shows me the ways to make the same lip gloss look like different colors by using different lip liners. Then she shows me how to put on eyeliner, eye shadow, and mascara. This is something my mother would have showed me how to do. I am sad and my eyes water just a little, but Maria thinks it's because she poked me with the eyeliner. "Sorry, I've never actually put it on someone. Here." She hands me the pencil. "I don't want to stab you again."

The first time I do it myself, I look like a raccoon. The second time, I get it right and I want to keep it on all night because it looks so pretty. Maria makes me wash it off. She says it's bad to sleep in makeup and we can do it again tomorrow.

"You want the top or bottom?" Maria asks me.

"Bottom."

"Good. I love sleeping on the top."

"Why?"

"I like being up high." Maria climbs up the ladder. I turn off the light and get into bed. "Serenity?"

"Uh-huh?"

"What do you want to be when you grow up?"

I want to say something that sounds important, but I don't really know yet what I want to be. "I don't know."

"Really? I want to be a singer." Maria sits up in the bed. "I have my plan all figured out—I will get discovered singing in church and be asked if I want to sign a recording deal. Of course, I'll say yes and then my song will hit the charts at number one and I will go on tour. After I get tired of the spotlight, I'll marry Ricky and we'll settle someplace where the paparazzi can't find us so our children don't grow up crazy because of all the hype." Maria is talking fast and barely takes a breath between words. Then she pauses and says, "Serenity, you should get a boyfriend so we can go out on double dates. Who do you have your eye on? Anyone here at camp?"

"Why do people keep asking me that?"

"Well, you never talk about boys. Who is the last person you kissed?"

"The last person I kissed was my grandma when I kissed her good night," I say, laughing. "If you mean a boy, well, I've never kissed a boy."

"What? You can't be serious!"

"I swear."

"Okay, we've got to get you a boyfriend. And we've got to make sure he has kissable lips."

"Kissable lips?"

"You know, not too big so they don't swallow you up and slobber all over your mouth. Not too thin, so you at least feel them against yours. Not chapped or cracked so they don't scrape you, and not busted or bloody for obvious reasons."

"So I guess that means Ricky has kissable lips?"

"Ricky's lips are the best lips ever."

"What is kissing like?"

Maria thinks to herself for a moment. "Well, it *tastes* kind of salty. It *feels* . . . well, I don't know. It's better than your favorite thing," she explains. She flings her head down from the top bunk and all I can see are her teeth. "Kissing is better than the best meal you've ever tasted." She smiles the biggest smile she's ever smiled. And I think this is Maria telling me she loves Ricky. She laughs at herself and then I laugh at her too. "Why haven't you kissed anyone?" Maria asks me. I say I don't know when really I think it's because I am not her.

• • • • • • •

Maria and I must have fallen asleep talking. I don't remember the last thing we said but I know we never said good night. It is morning now. After breakfast we have morning devotion. We are divided, boys in one room and girls in another. Pastor Mitchell's wife, Mrs. Mitchell, is our leader.

"Good morning, beautiful women of virtue," Mrs. Mitchell calls out. She looks like she has been up for hours. She has on a full face of makeup, her hair is perfectly curled, and she is the only one who does not give in to a yawn every now and then. "How are the daughters of Zion doing today?" Mrs. Mitchell always addresses us with what she calls affirmations. She says every day labels are put on us that are false and we need to hear what God says about us.

Mrs. Mitchell motions for Erica and Miss Valerie to come up to the front of the room. "We are very blessed to have Erica and Valerie with us for the weekend," Mrs. Mitchell says. "Young ladies, these are two women you need to be looking up to. I know there are tons of celebrities you all admire, but let me tell you, I've known these women since they were your age and believe me, they are great examples of what it means to be a woman of virtue."

Mrs. Mitchell always brags about Erica and Miss Valerie. We've heard this speech a thousand times. "Both of these young women did so well in high school they were awarded full-tuition scholarships to college," Mrs. Mitchell tells us. And she tells us how when Erica and Miss Valerie were our age they sang in the choir and passed the Rites of Passage and how if they can make it, we can.

Then Mrs. Mitchell announces, "We're going to have small group sessions today. Erica is going to lead one group and Valerie is going to lead the other."

Thank God Maria and I are put in Erica's group. We follow Erica to a small room. She rearranges the folding chairs and we sit in a circle. "Before we begin, do any of you have questions or want to talk about something that's on your mind?"

I think Erica intended for us to ask questions about God, but all the girls in the group want to know about her wedding. Karen asks, "How did Ivan propose?" Another girl asks, "How do you know when you're in love?"

Maria says, "She knows because Ivan bought her that huge platinum and diamond ring. Who wouldn't love a man that got her something like that?"

"Okay, okay," Erica says. "First off, let's all raise our hand to speak." She sits down in a chair and becomes a part of our circle. "I'll say a few things about Ivan, but then we have to get to our lesson for the day." Erica crosses her legs. "I think what's important to know is that before I loved Ivan I learned how to love myself. And yes, I like my ring a lot. But that is not what makes me love Ivan. Just because someone buys you nice stuff doesn't mean they love you. You'll know a person loves you by the way he treats you. A person who loves you will respect you. He won't pressure you or try to get you to change who you are."

Erica smiles at us. "Now, we can talk more about love and dating at lunch. We're supposed to be talking about prayer," she says.

Maria smiles. "Well, let's *pray* for our boyfriends."

We all laugh.

Erica says, "I'm praying that none of you settle for less. Your worth is priceless. Never sell yourself short." Erica opens her Bible. She tells us that people make prayer seem like a difficult thing to do, but it is simply talking to God. "And you can talk to Him about whatever you want," she tells us. Then Erica reads from her Bible a story about young people who prayed and saw God work miracles in their life. Daniel, Shadrach, Meshach, and Abednego. She tells us about times she prayed for people in her family or for struggles she was having and how God answered her prayers. "Sometimes, it might seem like your prayers aren't being heard. But don't give up. Things don't always change right when we want them to," Erica says.

There is an easel with chart paper sitting at the front of the room. Erica writes on it with a black marker:

On a piece of paper, write down a prayer to God for a family member or friend.

She passes out small sheets of paper with envelopes and says, "I want you to take your time with this and really think about it. It can be as simple as you want it to be, or it can be something that you think is impossible. God is a big God who hears and answers all kinds of prayers," she tells us. "I want you to write your prayer request in private and I don't want you to share it with anyone. This is between you and God."

We end with a song. Because there are no instruments and Maria is standing next to me, I can hear her voice clearly. Her voice floats through the room, harmonizing with the rest of us, making us sound better. "Don't forget to bring your assignment to afternoon Bible study," Erica says as we leave.

We have one hour of free time and then lunch before afternoon Bible study. "Let's go find Ricky and Danny," Maria says. We walk to the game room and there they are, taking turns at the air hockey table. Danny and Ricky are competing. Jay is standing on the side of the table, waiting for his turn. Maria stands next to Ricky and starts chanting like a cheerleader. "My man is going to win, Danny, I hope you know that!"

"Whatever, Maria," Danny says. "Your boy ain't got nothin' on me." He hits the puck hard and it goes in. Ricky cusses and then covers his mouth, realizing he just cursed at a church camp.

Jay starts laughing. "And everyone is worried 'bout how I'm gonna act," he says. Jay is right. All the adults watch him like he can't be trusted. "What are you doing for the rest of the break?" Jay asks me.

"I don't know. Watch my brother beat you and Ricky," I say, smiling.

"You got jokes, huh? I bet Danny won't beat me."

"Whatever."

"Watch. You gonna owe me," Jay says.

"Owe you what?"

Jay shrugs his shoulders. "I don't know. I'll think of something."

"And if Danny wins?"

"I'll owe you something."

Maria hears us and gives me a look and then she smiles big like she did last night when she was talking about Ricky. "I'm going to go do my assignment," she says. "See you later." She walks away, giggling, and I hope Jay doesn't notice.

Ricky hits his puck against the slippery table. The red circle almost flies into Danny's slot, but Danny quickly stops it and hits it hard, sending it back to Ricky's side and it goes in. "Dang it!" Ricky shouts.

"My turn," Jay says. He looks at me. "Sure you wanna watch?"

"Ha-ha." I stand there, waiting for Danny to beat Jay, but this time he loses.

Danny steps back from the table. "Your turn," he says to Ricky. "I'll catch up with you guys at lunch. Ivan wanted to talk to me about something." He walks away.

Ricky takes Danny's place. "All right, I'm 'bout to make a comeback." He starts another game with Jay. Jay scores first.

Before Jay can say anything to me, I say to him, "Don't gloat."

"Who me?" Jay smiles and I know I am staring at him, but I can't help it. "No need to brag just 'cause I beat him and I get you."

"You *get* me?"

"Yeah, I get you to do somethin' for me."

I have my hands on my hips and I feel Erica's and Maria's voices rise in me. "What is it that you want me to do?"

"Come on a walk with me." He scores against Ricky. "Tonight, after dinner."

"I'll think about it."

"Hey—I won the bet. You have to do somethin' for me, or in this case, with me." The red disk almost makes a goal for Ricky.

"You better watch what you're doing," I say.

"Got my eyes on you. Your beauty is distracting." Jay hits the disk hard. It flies off the table. Ricky runs to get it.

I can't believe he just called me beautiful. My face must be as red as that hockey disc. "I have to go," I tell him. "I have to do my assignment. See you later." I walk away.

Before I am even in the door to our room, Maria is

teasing me about Jay. "And you told me you didn't have your eye on anyone!"

"I don't."

"Serenity Evans, I know what I saw. You standing there, blushing. Jay flirting, trying to talk all smooth."

I sit down at the desk. "He wants to go for a walk tonight."

"See, I told you!"

"I don't think I should go."

"Why not? Are you crazy? Jay is *fiiiine*." Maria sits crossed-legged on the floor. "Why don't you want to go out with him? Maybe he'll ask if he can be your boyfriend."

"He didn't say he wanted to be my boyfriend. He said he wanted to go for a walk."

"Well, he doesn't want to go on a walk for exercise. I'm pretty sure he likes you. Don't you think he's cute?"

"Yeah. He's real cute. But I don't know. He's into things I'm not into." I give Maria a look and she knows what I'm talking about. All I can think about is that scripture Grandpa said to Danny. First Corinthians 15:33.

"You should get to know him. At least give him a chance. Maybe it will turn into something. Then you, me, him, and Ricky can all go out on a double date." Maria stretches her legs out and kicks off her shoes.

"My grandmother doesn't let me date yet."

Maria shakes her head at me. "Serenity, one sin isn't going to send you to hell. Look at it this way—if you disobey your grandmother, you'll have something to repent for. Don't you want to experience God's grace?" Maria bursts out laughing and so do I. She gets on her knees, like people do when they are called to the altar for prayer at church. "Lord Jesus," Maria shouts, mocking Mrs. McGee. "Forgive us, Father! Take this disobedience and lust out of our hearts! Purge our souls, Father, God!"

I play along with her. "Yes, Lord! Hallelujah!"

Maria gets up and starts doing a fake praise dance. She is jumping and turning in circles, waving her hands in the air, pretending to have *The Spirit*. We are laughing so hard tears are in both our eyes.

We finally stop fooling around and write our assignment. I want so bad to ask Maria what she is praying for, but I know it's none of my business. Besides, if I ask her, then she will want to know what I am asking for and I don't want to tell her. So I just keep quiet and write: *Dear God, please help Jay become a better person. And please help him to stop selling drugs.* I tuck my paper in the envelope and slide it in my Bible. I bet no one prayed for my dad. Maybe no one is praying for Jay either.

Afternoon Bible study is coed. I feel bad for not being able to concentrate. I am trying to focus, but all I can think about is Jay. Pastor Mitchell is telling us, "Young people, you are never too young to make a difference."

Then my mind wanders again to First Corinthians 15:33. I can't be a hypocrite and start hanging out with Jay when I've yelled at Danny for being his friend. I can't sneak off with Jay tonight. What will people think of the pastor's granddaughter going off with some boy that doesn't even go to church?

Pastor Mitchell is pacing through the aisles. "You can make a difference at school and in your neighborhood. When your peers are teasing someone or gossiping about somebody, you can stand up for what is right. That's how you show God's love."

Even though I am looking at Pastor Mitchell, I am not paying full attention. What if Jay tries to kiss me? What if we get caught like Maria and Ricky? My grandmother would pass out and go into a coma. I can't. I won't. I came here for God, not for boys.

"I want you all to come up to the altar," Pastor Mitchell says. All the youth flood the altar. "We're going to pray for the things you wrote down this morning."

Pastor Mitchell is standing at the front of the room. He looks at us and says, "Young people, no matter how simple your desires are, God wants to answer your prayers. What do you need God to do for you? What do you want? Let's take it to the Lord in prayer." He closes his eyes and begins to pray. I look over at Jay. His eyes are shut tight and it looks like he is really praying. I wonder what Jay needs from God.

Finally, Pastor Mitchell says "Amen" and dismisses us. We have an hour till dinner. Maria rushes off with Ricky and a smile on her face. Danny is talking to Ivan. I go to the game room to try to find Karen and Sabrina.

We are going to play board games until it's time for dinner.

"Wait up!" Jay yells. He jogs toward me. "You ready to go?"

"Where?"

"On our walk." He takes my hand and chills rush up my whole body. I quickly take my hand out his grasp, as if I've been shocked by something electrical or touched a hot stove.

"Ahh, it's like that. You don't want to hold my hand?"

"I have to go," I say.

Jay just smiles at me. "Next time, then," he says.

I walk away feeling proud. First Corinthians 15:33. I didn't give in.

AS IT IS

· · · · · · · · · ·

Serenity Evans
Mrs. Ross, 1st Period
Poetry Workshop

Anaphora: *When the beginning of the line repeats. Write a poem using the anaphora "I believe."*

I believe love is the medicine that cures fear.
I believe my grandparents' love
is a healing balm.
I believe some secrets need to be told.
I believe in second chances.

I believe change is possible, but I know change isn't easy.

We've been back from the retreat for a week now. It's Saturday morning and I wake up to the sound of slamming doors and yelling voices. Grandpa is standing at the foot of the steps screaming at Danny. "Young man, get back down these stairs right now!"

I hear Danny open the door, but he doesn't go downstairs. He is standing in the hallway yelling back at Grandpa. "What do you want? You've already said no. What else do we need to talk about?" Danny has found new boldness today.

I get out of bed and go into the hallway. "What's the matter?"

Danny snaps at me. "None of your business! Leave me alone."

Grandpa keeps fussing. "Danny, you don't walk away from me when I'm talking to you. And you don't slam doors and throw tantrums in this house. You understand?"

"Yes. But what I don't understand is why I can't get the shoes!"

Grandpa sighs. "Didn't I just get you shoes at the beginning of the school year?"

"Yeah, but those are ugly."

"Danny, the answer is no. No new video games, no new shoes." Grandpa starts to walk away. "You ought to be grateful for what you have. There are kids in this world who wish they had even one pair of shoes." Grandpa is out of sight now. He's walked toward the kitchen, still mumbling about how ungrateful the youth of today are and how materialistic we've become.

Danny is mumbling too. "My daddy would've got them for me," he says. But not low enough, because Grandpa is making his way up the steps before Danny can say anything else.

"What did you say?" Grandpa is short of breath because he is talking and walking up the steps at the same time. "You're right. Your father got you every *thing* you wanted. But, son, I'm going to give you what you *need*." When Grandpa reaches the top of the stairs, Danny backs up. Fear has come now and erased the boldness and attitude. He flinches and puts his hands out to protect his face.

"What are you flinching for? Why are you jumping back?" Grandpa is yelling loud. His voice is like thunder, an unexpected roar.

Now Grandma is at the foot of the steps, "James, leave him be. Leave him be," she says.

"Why did you just flinch up like that, huh? Answer me."

"James." Grandma is coming up the stairs too.

"Answer me."

Danny doesn't sound angry anymore. Now his voice is soft and low. "I thought you were going to hit me."

Grandma is upstairs now. The hallway seems tiny with the four us standing here. The silence is loud. No one speaks or moves until Grandma puts her hand on my grandpa's back. "Leave him be, James," she says softly.

Grandpa gently touches Danny on his shoulder. "Like I said, I'm not your father." He keeps his hand on Danny's shoulder and it must feel like a heap of coals because Danny's anger melts away and now he is crying. Grandpa repeats himself. "Son, I'm not your father. I'm not like him." Grandma gives me a look and so I go back in our room. I hear her walking down the stairs. Danny and Grandpa are still in the hallway. Neither of them say a word. All I can hear is the sound of crying. From both of them.

· · · · · · ·

Ricky comes over later. I try to stay out of their way, but every now and then I have to go upstairs to get something out of our room. I know Danny and Ricky are up to trouble because when I knock they both say, "Just a minute!" And it takes them forever to let me in. When I step in this time Danny is on the phone. I hear him say, "All right, Jay, we'll meet you at the park."

I am trying so hard to mind my own business. I just need to get my pad of paper and a pen and go back downstairs. I promised Grandma I would help her with the cookbook—but only the writing part. I'm going to take notes as she cooks so that we make sure she includes all the right ingredients and measurements. Grandma is one of those cooks that use a little bit of this and a little bit of that. She has never followed a written recipe. I close the door and Ricky says, "You sure you want to do this?"

Danny says, "Yeah. I need the money."

My heart is pounding and I think maybe I should go back in the room and ask them what they're up to, but I know they won't tell me. I go downstairs and whisper a prayer. God, please don't let them get in trouble.

I stay in the kitchen helping Grandma for most of the afternoon. "Your handwriting is so pretty," Grandma tells me. She is happy I am with her and it feels good to be wanted. "We've got to finish up," Grandma says. "Erica will be here soon. We're going to look at places where we can have the wedding and reception."

We clean the kitchen and now we have dinner for the next few days. Grandma plans to have four sections in the book: breads, main courses, side dishes, and desserts. "Next time we cook," she says, "we'll work on desserts. But we can't keep those in the house. Maybe Ricky's mom would like a pie."

"And Maria's too," I tell her. I don't know anyone who'd turn down my grandma's cooking.

When Danny comes home from the park, Grandpa fixes our plates and the three of us sit at the dining room table eating and talking about what we're going to do for

Halloween. The church is having a Harvest Festival. "Pastor Mitchell is planning lots of fun stuff for you all. Make sure you invite your friends." Grandpa gets up and puts his dishes in the dishwasher. "Danny, I was thinking. How about we compromise? You do some work around the house and at the church and I'll pay you an allowance so you can start saving up for those shoes and games and whatever else the mall has for you." Grandpa is smiling.

Danny gets up from the table, empties his dish, puts it in the dishwasher, and says, "How much?"

"Well, it depends. Five dollars a chore maybe. I don't know."

"Five dollars?" Danny heads upstairs. "That's okay, Grandpa. By the time I save up enough I'll be out of college and I'll be able to get a real job." Danny is smiling, but there is a little trace of attitude in his voice.

Grandpa laughs. Like a lawyer who is negotiating, he tells Danny, "Well, the offer is on the table, so whenever you're ready to take it, let me know." Then he looks at me. "You too."

"Okay," I say. And I think I'll take him up on his offer. Maria's birthday is next month and I want to get her something nice.

I go upstairs and get ready for bed. "Why don't you want to get paid for chores?" I ask Danny.

"I got it all worked out," he says. "Ricky and Jay are hooking me up."

"Doing what?"

"If I tell you, you're going to be mad and run and tell Grandpa."

"I promise I won't."

"You promise?"

"Yes, Danny. What is it?"

"Serenity, if you tell I'll never talk to you again."

"Danny!"

"All right." Danny goes into his drawer and pulls out a bundle of plastic cards that are wrapped in a rubber band. "You know how much money these are worth?" He hands me the cards.

I take the rubber band off and look at them. They're gift cards from just about every department and clothing store a mall could have. "What are you doing with these? Did you steal these?"

"No!" Danny whispers. He closes the door. "Okay, so here's how it works. Jay's cousin is a booster. She steals clothes and all kinds of stuff from stores and resells it to people."

"But how did she get these?"

"Let me explain!" Danny sits down on his bed. "She steals, like, five hundred dollars worth of clothes, or whatever, and then brings them back to the store, saying they don't fit." Danny lowers his voice even more. "But at most stores you need a receipt to take something back in order to get cash back. So instead they give her store credit on a gift card." Danny takes the cards out of my hands and shuffles through them. "Then she sells the cards. So say this card has two hundred dollars on it. She'll sell it for one hundred fifty."

I sit down on my bed. "How did you get the cards?"

"Jay told her to let me and Ricky in on it."

I am regretting that I promised Danny I wouldn't tell. "What else Jay got you selling?"

"Nothing. I mean, one of his boys, Dwayne, asked if I wanted to run an errand for him—you know, deliver it—but I told him no."

Danny can tell that I'm not for this. He goes into the bathroom and changes into his pajamas. When he comes out of the bathroom, I am waiting for him. "Danny, you can't do this."

"I knew I shouldn't have told you," he says. He tries to walk past me, but I won't move.

"Danny, you can't do it. It's wrong."

Danny tries to pass me again. I won't move. "Get out of the way," he yells.

"No."

"Serenity, move!" And then he pushes me. Hard.

I fall down and even though I'm not hurt at all, I don't get up. Danny stands there staring at me. He is breathing heavy and his eyes are teary, but he's holding it in.

"What's all the commotion?" Grandpa yells from downstairs. "Did somebody fall?"

I stand up. "I'm okay, Grandpa," I say. "I'm fine."

I step aside. Danny walks into the room.

I turn the lights off and get into my bed.

No knock-knock or Laffy Taffy jokes tonight. Just silence.

I can't help but worry. I think maybe I need to pray harder. And then I think, maybe prayer isn't going to work on Danny or on Jay. Maybe I just have to accept that some people don't change. I am so confused. I have been thinking that Jay isn't a bad person. Now I find out all this.

I feel really stupid. I was just telling Maria that I was finally going to go on a walk with Jay. Ever since we came back from the youth retreat, he's been asking about it. I've been feeling bad for avoiding him, but now I'm thinking that maybe Erica is right. Boys like Jay don't change. He's like those items on discount in stores that are going out of business, you have to take him as is.

IN HEAVEN

· · · · · · · · · ·

Serenity Evans
Mrs. Ross, 1st Period
Poetry Workshop

> **Personification**: *Making inanimate objects*
> *act like a person or animal: The fog crept in*
> *on little cat feet. Write a line of poetry using*
> *personification.*

Heaven smiled at me today.

I don't mind sharing a room with Danny, but Grandma
insists that I should have my own. "You're a woman now,"

she says. I am proud and happy and scared all at the same time. Grandma is going to tell Grandpa to turn his office into a room for me. She promises she won't say why. I can't wait to tell Maria. Now we are tied. Even though she has dated and kissed more boys than me, today I became a woman.

I take a shower after Grandma leaves the bathroom. I dry my body off, get dressed, and stand in front of the full-length mirror. I look like my momma today. Everybody has been telling me, but now I see it too. I don't realize I'm crying till Danny starts banging on the door.

"You fall in the toilet or something?" Danny is turning the knob.

"Just a minute." I wipe my tears and take one last look at myself. I can't believe it's happened. I open the door. Danny doesn't notice anything new about me. Not even my red eyes.

· · · · · · ·

My new room is the best room in the house. Grandpa painted it lavender and Grandma made white curtains for the windows. Grandpa put the glow-in-the-dark stars on the ceiling that I got with the money I earned doing chores. When the light goes out, my room becomes the night sky. Grandpa also put the plaque of my momma's favorite scripture on the wall beside my mirror. Everything in my room looks perfect. "Grandma, can Maria come spend the night?"

"Not on a school night, sweetheart. She can come this weekend." Grandma is in the kitchen doing inventory of her spices. She is wearing her reading glasses because the print on the bottles is so small.

I run to the phone and call Maria. "My grandma said yes. You can spend the night this weekend." We make plans on what movies we want to rent and I tell Maria to bring the nail polish that I like. She has the best colors. She also has the best makeup. She gave me eye shadow, eyeliner, and lip gloss, and every morning she meets me in the girls' bathroom and helps me do my makeup. The first time Jay saw me, he couldn't stop staring. I wash it off after school, before I meet Danny at the flagpole.

Wednesday and Thursday pass so quickly, I can't even remember what happened. Today is Friday. Maria is coming over after school. Danny thinks it's not fair that I get to have overnight company, so Grandma and Grandpa promised that Ricky can sleep over next weekend. Grandpa also said he'd get an outdoor basketball hoop for the driveway so Danny can have something new too. Danny is so excited. It's all he talks about to Ricky. That and video games. Maria is trying her best to find a way to come over next weekend too, but I know Grandma is not having that.

When the bell rings, Maria meets me by the flagpole. "Where's your stuff?" I ask her.

"My mom is dropping it off. It was too much to bring to school. Plus, she wants to talk to your grandma about something." Maria gets distracted when she sees Ricky and Danny walking toward us. Her eyes change. She moves a strand of hair out of her face, smiles, and gives Ricky a hug. They hold on tight to each other. I think about Jay putting his arms around me like that. How would that feel?

"Grandpa's here," Danny says. He is lugging his backpack on one shoulder and it weighs his whole right side down. "Call me tonight," he says to Ricky.

"All right." Ricky leans in to kiss Maria, but she backs up.

"Not in front of Pastor James," she says. She waves good-bye and we walk to the car.

Grandpa is listening to the radio. He turns it down to say hello and asks us how our day went. After we answer him, he turns it back up. We don't say much on the way to my house, so as soon as we pull in the driveway and get inside Maria and I can't stop talking.

"Your room is so nice!" She sits on my bed, bouncing up and down. "Are you happy not to be with Danny anymore?"

"Not really. I mean, it didn't bother me that much," I say. "But I do like being able to set things up the way I like it."

Danny likes having his own room too. He doesn't have to worry about me nagging him to clean it. Since I've moved out, he's decorated the walls with magazine covers of his favorite NBA players. He has his video games stacked on a bookshelf in all sorts of ways. Some with the name facing out, some on their side, some upside down. His desk has papers and books scattered everywhere.

I sit next to Maria. Our feet dangle off the side of the bed. "Now that we're not in the same room, I can't keep up on what he's doing."

"What do you mean?"

I tell Maria everything Danny told me.

"You didn't know about that?" Maria shakes her head. "Everyone knows that trick." Maria doesn't sound like she thinks it's a bad thing.

"But what if they start selling—"

"You worry too much," Maria says.

Grandma stands at the foot of the steps, calling out to us. "Dinner is ready," she says. Grandma has cooked baked chicken, cabbage, and red beans and rice. We sit at the dinner table and just as Grandpa starts to bless the food, the doorbell rings.

It's Maria's mother, Isabel. "Sorry to interrupt," she says. "I got off work late."

"Don't apologize," Grandma says. "Come on over here and eat with us." Grandma makes Isabel a plate.

"Thank you, thank you," Isabel says.

When we are finished with dinner Grandma says, "You all go upstairs. We need to talk."

Danny, Maria, and I go upstairs after we put our

dishes in the dishwasher. "I wonder what my mom wants to talk to your grandparents about," Maria says as we climb the steps.

I look at Danny. "Go ahead," he says and opens his door.

We follow Danny into his room. I sit on the floor next to the vent and motion for Maria to join me. "What's going on?" she asks.

"You can hear everything right here," Danny tells her.

He leaves, trying to act like he's not just as nosy as us. I open the vent, sit on the floor, and listen. Maria lies on her stomach, propping her chin up by her hands, and listens too.

"I just don't know what to do with her," Maria's mother says. "I found these in her room. I don't know about that Ricky."

Maria sits straight up and goes to cursing. Then she tells me, "I only have them just in case."

Maria's mom goes on and on about how she needs a break. Her new boyfriend, Miguel, and Maria keep arguing and she doesn't know what to do. "I know girls need to be with their mothers, but I'm thinking about sending her with her dad," Isabel continues.

I have never seen Maria cry. She gets up and goes into the bathroom, slamming the door. I close the vent. "Maria?" I stand at the door. She doesn't answer. "Maria, open the door." It takes a while. A long while. I must say her name a million times before she opens the door. When

I step into the bathroom Maria is sitting on the toilet, arms crossed, heavy breathing, red eyes. I just stand there—shocked to see her looking this way. But then I remember how it feels to be crying in front of someone and how the last thing you want is to have them stare at you or ask you questions. I rip a few squares of tissue from the roll and hand it to her. "Here, it's softer than the kind they use at school."

She smiles and gives me the biggest hug she's ever given me. Bigger than the hugs she gives Ricky. And she starts crying in my arms. I don't know how long we stand like this, but it's long enough for her to get rid of all the tears that are inside of her. When she lets go of me, she is breathing calmly. Then she looks at me, half smiling, half disgusted, half embarrassed. "Oh my God, I got snot on you!" And we both start laughing.

I leave Maria alone so she can wash her face. Later that night, while we are painting our nails, she blurts out, "Sometimes I hate her. I just hate her."

I don't say anything. I don't even look up. I just keep painting my nails.

"I'll run away before I let her send me to that man." Maria waves her hands side to side so her nails can dry. "I refuse to let him touch me again," she says. Maria gets quiet after she says this. Like she didn't mean for these words to come out. But since they have, she just keeps talking. "My dad, he—"

She stops and starts over. "When I was little, my dad

would play this game with me whenever I spent the night at his house. It happened from when I was seven till I turned nine. I hate going over there."

I stop painting my nails. I look at Maria. My mind goes to thinking that Maria and I aren't all that different. Maria knows what it's like to suffer too. And even though I don't wish her pain, I'm glad I have a friend who knows what it's like to hurt. I think that's why she doesn't try to get me to talk. She knows that there are some types of sadness that can't be explained.

"You still hiding from Jay?" Maria changes the subject just like that. Like she has a remote control and got tired of what she was watching. She just switches the topic and she doesn't seem upset anymore.

"I'm not hiding from him."

"Yeah, right."

I'm not. I actually try to find him. I purposely walk past his locker on my way to class, even when I don't need to go down that hall. When he's not in class I watch the door to see if he'll come in late. And during recess, even though Maria thinks I'm listening to her, I'm really watching Jay run up and down the court playing basketball.

We get into bed.

It's late. The house is quiet and the noise from the outside has stopped. No honking horns or singing sirens. The only sound I can hear is the tick-tock of my clock. The minute hand moves steady and never changes. I wish my life could move that way.

I turn over from my stomach to my back because my arm is getting numb. As soon as I move, Maria says my name. "Serenity?"

"Sorry. Did I wake you?"

"No. I can't sleep."

"Me neither."

Maria sits up in the bed. She leans against the headboard. I am on my back, still under my thick blanket. "Serenity, did your father ever hit you?" Maria asks.

"He pushed me once," I tell her. "I tried to break up a fight between him and my momma. He sent me flying across the room."

"But he never left bruises?" Maria asks.

"Not the kind people can see."

Maria is quiet for a short moment; then she says, "She can't make me live with him. She can't." She cries for a while and I take her hand and hold it tight. She takes a deep breath three times, calming herself down.

"Does your mom know? Have you told her?" I ask.

"What's the point? She's not going to believe me."

"How do you know?"

"My mom doesn't trust me. If I tell her now, she'll think I'm just making it up because I don't want to live with him," Maria says.

"Maybe you can stay with us," I say.

Maria sits straight up. "No, Serenity. No."

"Why not?"

"You can't tell your grandparents about my dad. You can't. If we say that I don't want to stay with him, they're going to ask why. And I'm not telling them."

"But why?" I ask. "They can help you."

"They can't help me. All that's going to happen is that they're going to talk to my mom about it and she's going to think I'm a liar," Maria says. "And my dad is going to deny everything. He'll be angry that I said something and it'll just get worse." Maria lays back down. "Promise me you won't tell them."

I am quiet.

"Serenity—"

"I promise. I promise I won't tell them."

Just as I close my eyes to go to sleep, Maria says, "Sometimes I just want to go there."

"Where?" I ask.

"Heaven." Maria is pointing to the glowing stars on my ceiling.

"What do you think it's like up there?" I ask.

"Peaceful."

"Do you think we'll know each other? I mean, you know, will we still be friends once we get there?"

"Of course I'll know you. I'll be like, 'Ooh, Serenity girl, your wings are fly!'"

We laugh and keep talking till we both are almost asleep.

"Maria?"

"Huh?"

"You think any of this stuff that happens down here is a surprise to God?"

"No," she mumbles. "I think God knows everything. Heaven ain't surprised about nothing."

GIVE US

· · · · · · · · · ·

Serenity Evans
Mrs. Ross, 1st Period
Poetry Workshop

Sensory Detail: *Language that evokes the
five senses: seeing, smelling, hearing, tasting,
touching*

Use sensory detail to describe an emotion.

Betrayal
Betrayal is faded black.
It smells like a blown-out candle.
It sounds like a car that won't start.

It tastes like burnt toast.
It feels like falling flat on your bottom because
someone moved the chair
you thought was there.

I am the first person to get invited to Maria's birthday slumber party. She hands me the invitation before any other girls in the school get theirs. It's a yellow envelope with my name written in silver writing. I can tell that Maria's mother wrote it. The Y in Serenity has the same pretty curl that she writes when she signs her name, Isabel Mosley, on Maria's permission slips. Inside the envelope is a thick square card with all the information for the party—when, where, what time, what to bring.

"You want to come with me while I give the rest of these out?" Maria asks me. She hands me a stack of five invitations and we walk down the hallway. The first two invitations we give out are to Karen and Sabrina. The next three are for Lisa, Sommer, and Denise. I am surprised that Lisa and her shadows are getting one. "My birthday's in two weeks," Maria says. She looks at me and I give them each their invitation.

Lisa snatches the invitation from me. "Where's your party, Chuck E. Cheese's?" She tears the envelope open. I don't think she notices Isabel's fancy writing.

"No, it's at my house. It's a slumber party," Maria answers.

Lisa slides the invitation out of the envelope. "Good, because Sommer's birthday party was at Chuck E. Cheese's and that was, like, a total disaster. I mean, like, we're too old to be running around with little kids, eating fattening pizza and watching oversized puppets sing corny songs." Lisa talks about Sommer's party as if Sommer isn't even standing there.

Sommer looks at me and explains. "It rained that day. Hard to plan something fun for a November birthday," she says.

Lisa ignores her, "Yeah, well, that's why I always say I was born in the best month. August. No school. No rain. My party is going to be at Bullwinkle's."

"What's that?" I ask.

Lisa looks at me. "You've never been to Bullwinkle's? *Everyone* has been there," she says. "Bullwinkle's has putt-putt golf, video games, laser tag, all kinds of stuff. It's the best," she explains.

"It has pizza too. Like Chuck E. Cheese's," Sommer adds.

"My parents usually just do a cake," Lisa says. Then she links arms with Denise and Sommer. "Maybe you'll come in August, Serenity. If you make my Good Friend List by then." They walk away. Maria and I are left standing there. The envelope is crumpled on the floor. Maria picks it up and throws it in the silver trash can that's stuffed to the brim and about to overflow.

I don't ask right away. Guess I need to make sure Lisa is far enough down the hall so she can't hear me. "Why are you inviting them?" I ask. "You don't like them."

Maria laughs. "Of course I don't. Well, Sommer is sweet. Denise is okay too. But I can't stand Lisa."

"Then why is she coming to the slumber party?"

"Well, we have to have someone to play pranks on," Maria says. "And Lisa gives good gifts."

I laugh so hard my cheeks start to sting. We walk to the bathroom and do our after-school routine. I wash my face and put on lotion. Maria sprays herself with one of her fruity body splashes. "You want to come over to my house today?" Maria asks.

"I can't. We have our counseling appointment."

"Okay, well, maybe tomorrow."

"Yeah." We walk to the flagpole and wait for my grandpa with Danny and Ricky. Grandpa is late picking us up so we have to rush to our appointment and don't stop for a snack like usual.

I can tell Ann has been waiting for me and that we've lost time, because she gets right into it when I get to her office. "How has your week been?" she asks.

"Good. Very good." I tell Ann how I'm crying less and laughing more. How I have my own bedroom and how Maria got to spend the night. I tell her about being a woman now and how I got a bookmark from Miss Valerie because I remembered the Old Testament Books of the Bible. I leave out being worried about Danny and the secret I'm keeping about Maria because today I only want to talk about good things.

"That's wonderful, Serenity. Wonderful."

I keep telling Ann about the good stuff. I tell her about Maria's slumber party, leaving out the part about us planning to be mean to Lisa and her shadows. "This is the happiest I've ever felt," I say. "I never had happy times before."

"Really? You've never been happy? Never?"

I get quiet.

"Did you ever have happy times with your mother?"

It takes me a while, but I shrug and say, "I guess so."

"Can you tell me about one of them?"

I don't say anything.

"What is one of your favorite memories with your mother?"

Memories begin to come to me. They flash fast and I can barely keep up. Some of them I forgot about till now—like the summer trip we took to Seaside Beach. Danny and I buried my daddy in the sand up to his neck. I remember eating crab legs for the first time at a restaurant that looked over the ocean. It took me forever to eat because I couldn't pull the crab out of its shell easily. It was good, but I was still hungry afterward, so Momma took us to McDonald's on our way back to the hotel.

I think about playing in makeup with my momma, and Danny and me hiding from her under the kitchen table. I think about my momma coming in the bathroom to wash my back when I couldn't reach it.

I remember how if my daddy didn't come home Danny and I would sleep in our parents' king-size bed and even with the three of us in it, there was room to stretch out my feet and arms and pretend to make snow angels.

I remember going grocery shopping and picking out the ripest fruit, the freshest vegetables, the best cut of meat so Momma could work her magic in the kitchen. I remember helping her chop vegetables, season meat, set the timer, mix the batter, grease the pan.

"My happiest time with my momma was helping her cook," I say. And even though I am thinking about the happy times, I am crying.

"See, you did have happy times. I bet you had lots more, huh?"

I shake my head. "It's just that the last day was so bad. So horrible. It erased all the good stuff."

"Was the whole day bad? Can you tell me what was happening before your parents started arguing?"

I shake my head and start crying real hard. I hate this. I was happy before I came here. I hadn't cried all week, not even when Maria cried in my arms. I didn't cry when the excitement of womanhood wore off and my stomach started cramping. And now, here I am, snotty nose, red eyes. I don't like talking to Ann. Her voice is like sour candy. Her words sting and burn and they make my eyes water.

"It's okay, Serenity." Ann looks at the clock. "You know, it's important to remember the good times too. That day was just one day of your entire life. There were many days before that—some bad, yes, but I'm sure there were good days too. Try to remember those moments this week if you can. Okay?" She looks at the clock again and stands. "I'll see you next time. Have a great week."

When I get home I just want to go to my room. I want to turn off the lights and look at the ceiling. But Grandma has other plans for me. "Serenity, after you change out of your school clothes would you like to help me fix dinner?" Grandma is cutting onions and bell peppers for the meatloaf.

"Sorry, Grandma. I have to get started on homework. But I'll set the table," I answer.

"Okay, sweetheart. I'll call you down when it's ready."

Grandma is mixing the peppers, onions, and seasonings in the ground beef. Her wedding ring is sitting on the kitchen countertop. She only takes it off when she cooks messy things. Her fingers are knuckle-deep in the meat and she is mixing it and pounding it all together. Her back is to me and I think she knows I'm staring at her, but she doesn't turn around. I can't believe she isn't begging or insisting that I help her. I wait one moment more to make sure I've won. She keeps on kneading the meat. I go upstairs.

Danny is sitting in his room with the door wide open.

He's playing video games. I stand in the doorway. "You finished with your homework?" I ask.

He doesn't answer me.

I notice there are five new games sitting on his bed and he has two boxes of shoes by the closet. "Danny, did you do your homework?"

Danny still doesn't say anything.

"Danny, you better not start messing up in school. You know you're not supposed to play games till your homework is done."

"Why are you trying to be like Momma? Always telling me what to do, always checking on me. You're not my mother! Momma's dead, all right!" Danny slams his door.

For a moment I am frozen. I want to be mad at him, but I am mostly sad. I knock on the door. "Danny?"

He doesn't answer.

"Danny, I'm not trying to be like Momma. I just—"

"Leave me alone, Serenity," he yells through the door.

I go into my room. I lie on my bed, looking at the ceiling, and try to remember the things I've forgotten. I think about how when we were younger, Danny and I didn't argue as much as we do now. We would play all day in the summertime, riding our bikes and racing each other to the corner. We'd put on concerts for our momma, lip-synching to her old records.

We always shared a room, so at night we talked about everything. I remember one night we went to our room hungry because Momma couldn't afford real groceries that time, just packaged noodles and Kool-Aid mix. Danny told me that when he grew up and got a job he was going to make sure Momma always had enough money to do whatever she wanted. We promised we'd split the cost of a house so that Momma could live in a nice place and have a real big kitchen. For some reason, we just assumed Daddy wouldn't be there. Never thought about Momma not being there when we got grown.

· · · · · · ·

Maria and I have been counting down the days till her slumber party, and it's finally here. Isabel's boyfriend, Miguel, doesn't look too thrilled to have all these girls coming over. He fixes himself a plate of food and disappears into their bedroom. I barely get a glimpse of him. He's like a ghost. Making appearances and vanishing in the blink of an eye.

Karen and Sabrina are the first to arrive. "Come in. Maria's downstairs," I say. I feel important, like this is kind of my party too since I've helped plan everything.

"Be up in a sec!" Maria yells. Karen and Sabrina sit down on the sofa.

When Maria comes up the stairs she turns on music. Her playlist has merengue, reggaeton, bachata, salsa, and hip-hop. We all start dancing and Isabel takes pictures and laughs at us, saying she can't believe how us young people dance these days. We barely hear Lisa, Denise, and Sommer knocking on the door, the music is so loud. They come in looking like triplets with their matching hairstyles. Ponytails. Lisa's to the side, Denise's on top of her head, and Sommer's pulled back.

Maria rolls her eyes toward me and flashes a fake smile at them. "Hi, guys, I'm so glad you could make it." I can't believe how good of an actress Maria is. She should audition for our school play.

"Is anyone else coming?" Lisa asks. She surveys the room and doesn't sit down just yet, like she is deciding if she is going to stay or not.

"This is everyone, now that you're here." Maria is too joyful. It makes me laugh to watch Karen and Sabrina react to her. They've never seen her so nice, not even at church.

Lisa decides to stay, as if she's doing us a favor. By the time she finishes eating Isabel's cooking, she seems like she's having a good enough time. After we eat, we go to the basement and get to talking about boys.

"You know who I think is real cute?" Karen says.

We all say "Who?" in unison.

"Jay! He is the finest boy in the school."

"In the world," I blurt out. I hope I didn't just make it obvious that I like him. I don't think anyone notices because they just keep talking, but Maria looks at me and smiles.

"But you know who I think is even finer than Jay?" Lisa asks.

"Who?" we all ask again.

"Okay, don't laugh. I mean, I know he's younger but only by one grade." Lisa keeps making excuses. We beg her to tell us. "Well," she says. "Serenity, your brother, Danny, is *sooo* cute!" All the girls agree and then they start talking about Danny in ways I've never heard anyone talk about him before.

"Okay, okay, we're talking about my brother here. Please," I say.

Maria understands. She says, "If I had a brother, I'd make it a rule that none of my close friends could like him."

Lisa says, "Serenity doesn't need that rule for me. We're not close friends."

The room gets quiet and I feel embarrassed and angry and I look at Maria, who is now standing with her hand on her hip and yelling. "Why you gotta be so rude?"

Lisa says, "Well, you said the rule would be for close friends and me and Serenity aren't close, so I can date Danny if I want. That's all I meant." Lisa looks at me. "Really, that's how I meant it. I like you, I do. I was just telling Denise and Sommer that I think I'll invite you to my birthday party."

What makes her think I'd even want to go? I can't wait to put itching powder in her sleeping bag tonight.

Isabel comes into the basement just at the right time and says, "Maria, let's open your gifts."

Maria rolls her eyes at Lisa and changes her voice to

the sweet, innocent one. "Okay." She walks over to the table where her gifts are stacked and opens Sommer's first. Sommer gets her a beauty kit: two kinds of lip gloss, two bottles of nail polish, and shimmer lotion that has glitter in it so it shines on your skin. Denise gets her an outfit: a pair of jeans and a cute light blue sweater. Karen and Sabrina went in together for their gift: a box of stationery that has Maria's name on it.

Maria opens Lisa's next. I think she is saving mine for last because she knows mine is going to be the best. Lisa's gift is big. It can't even fit on the table. It's on the floor beside the table, wrapped perfectly in pink and white paper with a fancy silver bow on top. Maria is careful as she opens it. "This paper is so pretty, I'm going to save it." I can't tell if Maria is being her sweet, fake self or if she really likes it. When she gets the paper off, we all see what the gift is. A karaoke set. "Oh my goodness! Mom, do you see this?" She opens the box, not neat this time, and starts taking everything out. "There's a song list," she says. "And look, Mom, a mike!" Maria is grinning wide. Her mother too.

Lisa smiles. "I know how you like to sing," she says.

"Thank you so much!" Maria gets up and hugs Lisa. Long. Tight. Like it means something real. Maria starts hooking up the karaoke machine. She forgets all about my gift. It's buried under that pretty pink and white wrapping paper she tossed all over the place.

I pull it from under the pile of paper while everyone

is helping her figure out how to work her new gift. I slide the gift in my pocket and realize that gifts that can fit in your pocket aren't that good of a gift in the first place. But I thought she'd like it. It's a silver locket, the shape of a heart, with a picture we took at the mall in a booth. Grandpa helped me scan the picture and cut it down to fit perfectly in the locket I bought with the money I earned doing extra chores.

"Serenity, what song should I sing first?" Maria shouts out. She is looking through the song list and the girls are sitting on the floor, like an audience. "Something fast," I say. A slow song would make me more sad right now.

And just like that, Maria is singing and the girls are clapping and she doesn't even remember any of the pranks we were going to play on Lisa and her shadows. She also forgets that she told me I didn't have to bring a sleeping bag because I'd get to sleep with her in her bed. Instead, Lisa is in her bed and I'm on the floor.

The next morning, I wake up before the others. I hear Isabel in the kitchen fixing breakfast. She promised Maria pancakes. "Good morning, Isabel."

"'Morning, Serenity." Isabel pours the batter into the frying pan. The phone rings. "Hello?" Isabel holds the phone between her neck and chin, pushing her shoulder up to keep it in place. "She's right here. The first one to wake up," Isabel says. She smiles at me. Her face morphs and becomes serious. "I see, I see. Okay, I'll tell her. Yes,

I'll make sure." She hangs up the phone. "Your grand-mother has to come pick you up early, okay?" She's put on that voice adults use when they talk to small children.

"Did she say why?"

"Ah, no. I—I don't know." She is not good at lying. "She'll be here in about twenty minutes," Isabel says.

I get dressed and get my bag. I wait by the door till Grandma comes to get me. Isabel fixes me a plate of food and tells me she'll tell Maria why I left. "Okay," I say. In a way, I'm glad I'm leaving early. The way Maria was act-ing last night, I don't even think she'll care that I'm gone.

I know what Grandma has to tell me is serious because she makes small talk the whole way home. Grandma doesn't waste words. She never talks about the weather or random things that people talk about when they are uncomfortable with silence.

I get nervous. What if Grandpa has had another heart attack? I look at Grandma. It can't be that. She's too calm.

When Grandma pulls up to the house, the first thing I notice is that Erica's car is parked in the driveway. When we step inside the house, I see that the TV screen is cracked and the living room is in a mess. Erica is clean-ing it up. Putting the pillows back on the sofa and set-ting the family pictures back up on the fireplace mantel.

I can hear Ivan's voice coming from my grandparents' room saying, "Danny, we know you're upset. You're hurt. And you have every right to be, but you can't destroy things. You can't throw fits like this."

I sit down. Grandma sits next to me and says, "Serenity, the police found your father this morning."

"Where?"

"In California," she tells me. "In his car, dead." She talks slow, real slow and gentle. "He killed himself, Serenity. Shot himself."

I look at the broken TV. Erica adds, "It's all over the news. We didn't want you to find out the way Danny did."

I think maybe I really have cried all the tears given to a person, because nothing comes out. I just sit there. I can't move, or talk. Just sit. There's a knock at the front door. I look out the bay window and see vans from news stations pulling up to our house. Grandma closes the blinds and doesn't answer the door.

"You want to talk about it?" Erica asks.

I just sit.

She rubs my back and then gets up. "Let me know if you do," she says. Then she sweeps the glass from Grandma's broken vase off the hardwood floor. She goes into the kitchen, where Grandma is and whispers, "I can't imagine what she's thinking."

I lean back against the sofa. What I'm thinking is, did my father kill himself because he was so guilty and ashamed of what he did that he just couldn't take it anymore, or did he do it because he was afraid of going to jail?

After Erica and Ivan leave, Grandma tries to get us to eat, but no one is hungry, including Grandma. She splits the homemade soup she made into two Tupperware bowls and freezes them.

Danny and I mostly stay in our rooms. I try reading, then writing, then drawing, but nothing can take my mind off my daddy. Our phone has been ringing all day. And reporters are standing outside with their cameras and microphones. I hear one of them say, "The tragic saga ended today . . . ," and I think, nothing has ended. Not the sadness, anyway.

I overhear Grandpa on the phone yelling and screaming, demanding an apology from the detectives because our family wasn't notified before it was on the news. His voice moves through the house like a furious tornado. On the next phone call, I hear him say, "No, our family has no statement at this time."

I get in bed and slide under the cover. I sleep through the night, but then I wake up from a nightmare at six o'clock in the morning. Even though I wasn't there to hear the gunshot, I hear it in my dreams.

I don't bother going back to bed. Everyone will be awake soon anyway. I go into the bathroom. Danny must've been in here. The toilet seat is up. I use the bathroom and wash my hands. I throw the paper towel in the garbage and see that the calendar Danny and I had on the wall is on the top of the trash. I pull it out. Danny's still been marking off the days. There are red X's up until today's date. The tears I thought I didn't have wash over me.

Daddy didn't come back for us. Didn't even say sorry.

I take the calendar downstairs and toss it in the fireplace on top of the wood and paper Grandpa has prepared to burn. I sit on the sofa, crossed-legged, and lean back on the soft pillows.

An hour passes and Danny comes down to the living room. He sits next me. I lean my head on his shoulder. We don't say anything. We just sit and stare at our reflection in the glass door of the fireplace.

"I knew he wasn't coming back," Danny mumbles.

"Me too," I say.

Is this how my momma felt all those times when she made herself believe my daddy would change, even though she knew he wouldn't? Sometimes you want something to be something else so bad that you just won't accept things the way they are.

"You two up already?" Grandpa says. Grandma comes out after him. She says "Good morning," and goes into the kitchen. "Honey, turn the heat on. The house is cold," Grandma calls from the kitchen.

Grandpa opens the door to the fireplace. Our reflections disappear. He starts a fire. The red and yellow flames rise high. Grandma brings me and Danny hot chocolate with marshmallows on top. She sets the mugs on the glass coasters on the coffee table. She and Grandpa sit in their armchairs, swapping pages of the morning paper and drinking coffee.

The four of us sit together watching the flames devour the paper and wood.

Danny drinks a little sip from his mug and asks real low, "Do you think Grandma Mattie will have a funeral for Daddy?"

"I don't know," Grandma says.

"If she does, I'm not going," I tell them.

"Me neither," Danny says.

Grandpa says, "You won't have to."

I think to myself, I hope she doesn't have a funeral. Then he'll be in a casket, all dressed up, looking nice. I hope he's cremated. If he's cremated, there will be no peaceful smile on his face like he's glad about everything that's happened.

• • • • • • •

The rest of the weekend is a blur. We don't go to church and Grandma says we can stay home from school if we want to, but both Danny and I decide to go. Mrs. Ross knows about everything so she is extra nice to me today, and when I tell her I don't have my assignment finished, she says I can turn it in tomorrow. Mrs. Wilson keeps looking at me with eyes of pity. She smiles at me when I pass her class and tells me if I ever need to talk to her, she's here for me. Like I would ever, ever talk to her.

I don't know if Mr. Harvey knows. I get to class just as the tardy bell rings and he gets started right away.

Maria sits next to me. We haven't spoken since her party. I want so badly to talk to her about my father. I need to. But my feelings about our friendship are all jumbled and messed up.

Mr. Harvey hands out a sheet outlining our next unit. "So we've finished our unit on Body Systems. Today we're starting a new unit, which is Growth and Development." When he passes out the last sheet of paper, he walks back to the front of the room. "We'll be discussing the different things you'll feel in your body and in your emotions now that you're a teen, and how to stay safe physically, mentally, and emotionally during adolescence."

I know this is Mr. Harvey's way of saying we'll be talking about drugs and sex and making good decisions. Just when he starts talking, there is a loud noise in the hallway. A thumping. Someone yells, "Fight, fight!" and everyone in Mr. Harvey's class runs into the hallway. We all form a semicircle, almost like we planned it. I am too short to see over the tall people.

Mr. Harvey is yelling. "All right, break it up. Break it up!" He pushes through us to get to the front of the circle.

I hear Maria's voice screaming, "Ricky, stop! That's enough. Danny, stop!"

I shove myself through the mob, and when I get to the front, I see Danny and Ricky kicking and punching some poor boy who is on the floor, bleeding from his nose and mouth. "Danny!"

Mr. Harvey, Principal Scott, and another teacher find

a way to pull Ricky and Danny off the boy. Principal Scott yells at the rest of us, "Go back to class. Get back to class. Now!" Most of us don't move. Everyone is talking about what they just saw. Giving each other play-by-plays. "Whoever does not return to class immediately will be getting a referral and be held in detention during tomorrow's lunch."

The group runs in separate directions and goes back to their classrooms. Maria and I follow Principal Scott. "Ladies, that means you too."

"He's my brother," I say. I look at Danny, fighting to get out of the grip of Mr. Scott's hold. Looking like Daddy did when the police came to arrest him the night the neighbors called. "He's my brother."

"Serenity, go back to class. I'm fine." Danny won't look me in the eye. He is breathing hard and there are a few scratches on his face. His shirt is torn at the neck.

"What happened?" I am running to keep up with them, following them to Principal Scott's office.

We pass the nurse's room on the way. The boy is there, holding a tissue to his nose. He yells out, "This ain't over! This ain't over!"

The nurse slams the door shut.

Principal Scott motions for Danny and Ricky to step into his office. He closes the door and turns to us. "You can wait out here. Serenity, please give Maggie the best number to call so we can arrange for your brother to be picked up. Maria, you need to get back to class."

Maria doesn't move. I step up to Maggie's desk. I give her the number to the church office. She calls and I hear her telling my grandpa that Danny was in a fight and I know that tonight is going to be a long night.

"You can go back to class now," Maggie says.

"Come on, Maria. Let's go."

Maria follows me out of the office. Lisa and her shadows are walking toward us when we step into the hallway. Maria asks, "Do you guys know why Ricky and Danny were fighting?"

Lisa tells us everything. "That boy was, like, totally disrespecting Danny. He was saying all kinds of things."

"What did he say?" Maria asks.

"Well—" Lisa looks at me. "He said he read in the paper that you and Danny were orphans."

"We're not orphans!" I am so mad I want to fight Lisa myself just for repeating it.

"That's what the fight was about. Ricky was sticking up for you guys. Telling that boy that you had a family, that you, like, live with your grandparents or something. But the boy said that didn't count. Orphans are kids who don't have parents. And then your brother got all mad and told the boy to stop disrespecting him but the boy wouldn't. I don't remember what the boy said that made your brother hit him, but the next thing I knew they were beating him up and stuff."

I can't stand here and listen to any more. I am mad that someone was teasing my brother and mad that Lisa

knows I don't have parents. I am just mad about everything right now. Especially at what a hypocrite Lisa is. As
she walks away with Sommer and Denise, she says, "I
understand why Danny fought him. I mean, like, that
boy has to learn that you have to give respect to get it.
You know?"

THIS DAY

· · · · · · · · · · ·

Serenity Evans
Mrs. Ross, 1st Period
Poetry Workshop

Metaphor: *a comparison without using*
like *or* as*: He is a big mean bear.*

Write a metaphor describing someone
you know.

Jay is the sun that shines
on a day when the weatherman forecasted rain.
He is a breeze blowing on a hot, humid day.

He is a mystery book
with an unexpected twist at the end.

Grandpa and Grandma can't come to get us after school today because Grandpa has a doctor appointment. I don't bother to wash off my makeup after school. Maria gave me a new color to try and it looks good on me. I don't want to take it off yet.

Before we left for school this morning, Grandma told me, "I'm trusting you to get home safe and on time, okay?" This is Danny's first day back at school since the fight. He was suspended for three days. He's on punishment for the rest of the month: no video games, no television, double chore duty.

I promise Grandma that I will look out for Danny and he promises not to give me a hard time. Maria is not in school today. I miss her all day long. I sit with Karen and Sabrina at lunchtime, but it's just not the same. At the end of the day, on my way to meet Danny at the flagpole, Jay walks up from behind me. "Haven't seen you in a while," he says.

I slow down and we walk together outside. "I've been here at school. Where have you been?"

"Takin' care of some things," Jay says. "Can I walk you home? You still owe me."

"You can walk me *and* Danny home," I say.

When we get outside, Ricky and Danny are standing under the flag talking. "What's up?" Jay says to both of them.

"Hey, Jay. Hi, Serenity," Ricky says. I haven't seen Ricky all week because he was suspended too.

I thank him for sticking up for my family and we all start walking. Ricky only lives a few blocks from us so we are walking the same way. Usually he spends time with Maria after school, but since she's not here today, he's with us. He walks beside Danny, and I am glad Danny has a good friend. Ricky is like a brother. Especially since the fight. Everyone knows it too. You mess with Danny, you'll have to deal with Ricky. You mess with Ricky, you'll have to deal with Danny.

Jay is walking close to me. Our bodies sometimes brush against each other when we walk through tight spaces, so I scoot over to give him more room. Danny and Ricky are ahead of us. They're having their own conversation. Ricky's bragging about how he was suspended.

Danny is in awe. "What? My grandfather had me doing all kinds of stuff. I had to rake the leaves from off the sidewalk and in the backyard."

"Man," Ricky sighs. Like Danny has it so tough.

"But that's not all," Danny adds. "I had to go to the church to clean the bathrooms and vacuum the sanctuary."

"That's crazy, man. I can't believe he had you doin' all that."

"And when I was done with that, he just made up stuff for me to do."

"Like what?" Ricky asks.

"Like shredding papers, doing inventory on how many Bibles and hymnals we have in the pews."

"Man, Pastor James don't mess around, huh?"

"He's real strict," Danny says. "My grandmother is too."

"I always wondered what it would be like being a PK."

Danny switches his backpack to his left shoulder. "It sucks. It's even worse being the brother of a goody-two-shoes." He turns around and gives me a look.

"Shut up, Danny!"

"Make me!"

I run up and hit him in his arm.

"I was just messin' with you!" Danny says. But I don't believe him.

Ricky is laughing. Jay slows his pace down and takes my hand. "Don't let him get you mad."

"I'm not thinking about him," I say. How can I now that Jay is touching me? Our fingers lock into one another's like two puzzle pieces. I don't let go.

We fall way behind Danny and Ricky and it's too hard to hear what else they are saying. I am uncomfortable walking in silence with Jay so I try to start up our own conversation. "So when are you going to start coming to church?" I ask. It's the only thing I can think of. Maria would probably be real disappointed in this. I can just hear her say, "Of all the questions to ask him, you asked him that?"

"I don't know," Jay answers. "I liked the camp thing we went to. I might come one day."

I tell him about our Rites of Passage ceremony. "You have to come to that. Maria and I will be speaking. And Maria's going to sing a solo."

We keep walking, and the closer we get to my house, the more I want to slow down. We get to Ricky's corner and he says good-bye. After two more blocks, we are at my house.

"All right, man. I'll see you tomorrow." Danny goes into the house. I stay outside with Jay. I know Danny is going to make a big deal out of this when I get inside.

Jay pulls his cell phone out and checks the time. I snatch it from him. "What do you need a phone for?"

"So I can call you," Jay answers.

"Whatever." I sit down on the top stair of the porch. Jay sits next to me.

"I'm serious. Can I call you tonight?"

I try to think of something clever to say, something to make it seem like I'm playing hard to get, but the truth is the only thing I can think of. "I'm not allowed to have boys call the house for me," I say. Maria isn't going to believe I actually told him this.

Jay looks at me. His eyes are so brown, so perfectly brown, they are looking at me and I want to melt because

I have never been looked at like this. "Okay. I don't want you gettin' in trouble." Jay steps off the porch.

What would Maria do? "But you can give me your number and I'll call you," I say.

Jay smiles.

I take my notebook out of my backpack and tear out a sheet of paper. I hand it to him with a pen. Jay writes his number down and gives the paper back to me. "Thanks for letting me walk you home," he says.

"Thanks for walking me." I give Jay a hug. I want to stay in his arms, have him hold me tight.

He lets go. "See you later," he says.

My legs feel like they might not be able to hold me up much longer. I sit back down on the porch and watch him walk away.

Once night comes and everyone is asleep, I sneak the cordless phone in my room and call Jay. He talks to me for hours and no matter how strong my eyes burn or how many times I yawn, I stay on the phone. I could listen to Jay's voice all night long.

OUR DAILY BREAD

· · · · · · · · · ·

Serenity Evans
Mrs. Ross, 1st Period
Poetry Workshop

Hyperbole: *An exaggeration.*
Thanksgiving hyperboles

1. The turkey in the school's cafeteria was so hard, I couldn't cut through it with a jackhammer.
2. Grandma cooked so much food, we'll be eating leftovers for the rest of our lives.
3. It rained so hard on Thanksgiving Day, I thought Noah was going to float by in his ark.

The shelter is full today, as usual. Before anyone can eat, they have to attend a short worship service upstairs in the sanctuary. Grandpa ends in prayer and sends the homeless downstairs.

Grandma and I are waiting in the kitchen. I am helping serve today because I want to start collecting hours toward my community service goal for the Rites of Passage requirements. My other community service project is designing holiday cards to give away to people at the shelter when we serve them on Christmas Eve.

A woman comes up to the table dressed in a dingy white dress. She has on sandals, and the left shoe has a broken strap. "Who we got here, Mrs. Claire? You done hired you some help, I see." The woman holds out her plate. I am serving the meat. I give her one slice of turkey and a slice of ham. Karen and Sabrina are serving the side dishes. They scoop out big helpings of stuffing, macaroni and cheese, and string beans.

"That there is my grandbaby. She'll be coming once a week in the evenings now." Grandma sounds happy, like she's been wanting me to come all along. "Introduce yourself, baby." She looks at me.

"Hi, my name is Serenity. Nice to meet you."

"Nice to meet you too. I'm Thelma," the woman says. "And who are these two young ladies?" Karen and Sabrina say their names at the same time and start laughing at how they just jinxed each other. Ms. Thelma holds her plate out to Karen and Sabrina, grabs a napkin, walks away, and sits at the table closest to the assembly line. When she takes a bite of her food she shouts, "Mrs. Claire, you a saint. You know what them other places be servin' us?"

A man in a green shirt and torn shorts blurts out, "Mush!"

Someone else adds, "They call it soup."

"Ain't fit to feed a dog," Ms. Thelma says. "We appreciate you, Mrs. Claire. Thank you."

Grandma says, "I guess I just don't know how to cook no other way. I'm just doing what I know how to do." Grandma doesn't like people to fuss over her. She always gives the glory back to God. People ask her all the time how she gets the money to feed people all this good food. Grandma always tells them, "The Lord provides." But I know that besides the benevolent offerings at church, and the donations from local stores, Grandma pays for a lot of it out of her own pockets. She changes the subject away from herself and asks the people at the table, "Have you all signed up for our transitions class?"

"Sure have!" The man in green holds up his brochure. Our church has a ministry called Transitions. It's to help the homeless get back on their feet.

The line is steady coming for almost two hours and then it slows down. I look out at the crowd. There are three young girls sitting with a woman who has a black eye. "Stop staring," my grandma says to Karen and

Sabrina. Grandma hands Karen a tray of small bowls filled with banana pudding. "Pass these out, please."

After dessert is served and everyone leaves, I help Karen and Sabrina clean up. They wipe the tables, I sweep. "It was kind of sad seeing all those people today," Karen says.

Sabrina agrees. "I know. Especially the mothers and children."

"I wonder where their fathers were," Karen asks.

I sweep the last bit of dust in the dustpan. "Maybe they don't have fathers."

"Everyone has a father," Karen and Sabrina say at the same time. They laugh. "We jinxed each other again!" They can't stop laughing.

I don't say anything. I just watch them laugh and I sit down in one of the metal folding chairs. Karen and Sabrina don't understand what it's like to have parents who don't know how to be a mother or a father. Their parents are married and their dads and moms come to all their school performances. When our class went on a field trip to a museum downtown, Karen's and Sabrina's dads chaperoned. I told Ann about them and how I think it's not fair that God would give me a horrible dad but give them good ones.

Grandpa comes to pick us up from the church. On our way home we stop at Ricky's house to get Danny. He spent the night over there after hours of begging and pleading.

"Serenity, go ring the doorbell and let him know it's time to go," Grandpa says.

"Okay." I open the door.

"And thank Ricky's mom for me, please," Grandma says.

I run up the grass to Ricky's house and ring the doorbell. Ricky's younger sister opens the door. She's seven years old and she always says my name wrong. "Hi, Ren-i-ty."

"Hey, Cocoa. I'm here for my brother."

"He's gone with Ricky."

"Gone where?"

She shrugs.

"Where's your mom?"

"In Seattle."

"What do you mean, she's in Seattle?"

"She's with her boyfriend in Seattle," Cocoa says. "But Tasha is here," she tells me.

Tasha is Ricky's sixteen-year-old sister. Cocoa knocks on Tasha's bedroom door. Tasha comes out, rubbing her eyes and yawning. "Hey, Serenity. What's up?"

"I'm looking for my brother."

"He's not here? I thought he was in Ricky's room."

"Ricky's not here either," I tell her.

"What?" Tasha goes to Ricky's room and opens the door.

"I'll be back," I tell Tasha and Cocoa. I know my grandparents are going to ground Danny for the rest of his life. I walk back to the car, and before I reach it, Grandma is rolling down the window. "Um, Danny and Ricky aren't here right now," I tell her.

Grandpa says, "Did Ricky's mom say where they went?"

"Um, Ricky's mom isn't here either." I could've lied, but I don't want to get in trouble. "I can call Maria. Maybe they're over there."

Grandpa turns off the car and tells me to go call. Grandma gets out of the car and comes in the house to speak with Tasha. While they talk, I call Maria. Her mother picks up. "Hi, Isabel. This is Serenity."

"Serenity? I haven't seen you since the party. Don't be a stranger."

"I won't," I say. "Is Maria home?"

"No. Not right now. She went out with ah, oh, what's that girl's name? I can't remember." Isabel thinks for a moment—"Linda?"

My heart sinks and I just want to slam the phone down. "Lisa? She's with Lisa?"

"Yes, that's it. They went to the movies. You want me to tell her you called?"

"No, that's okay. You don't have to."

"All right, *Mami*. See you at church tomorrow."

"Bye, Isabel." I hang up.

By the time I'm off the phone, Grandma has used Tasha's cell phone to call Ricky's mom and tell her what is going on and Cocoa is bundled up in her coat. She's coming with us. Tasha looks part relieved, part scared. She keeps apologizing to Grandma. Grandma says, "It's not you I'm upset with, honey."

When we get to the car, I help Cocoa with her seat belt. "Well?" Grandpa says.

"They're not with Maria," Grandma tells him.

"What are we going to do with this boy?" Grandpa starts the car.

"He might be with Jay," I say.

Grandpa pulls out into the street. "Let's see," he says when he reaches the corner. "I think he lives this way." He turns on his left blinker.

"No, Grandpa. Make a right." I know exactly where he lives. Maria showed it to me once. Ever since then, I've walked the long way back from the corner store just to walk by his house, praying that he'd be outside. Whenever he is, I stop and we talk for a little bit. Jay always gives me a compliment about something—my hair, my outfit. Last week he told me I had a pretty smile. I must have smiled for the rest of the day.

We ride in the car, Grandma humming the whole time. "Pull over here, Grandpa." There it is. Jay's house. Please, God, please let them ask me to go ring the doorbell again. They don't. Grandpa gets out of the car. As he is standing on the porch knocking, I see a group of boys walking from down the block. "There they are," I tell Grandma.

Danny and Ricky are walking with four other boys.

I see Jay in the back of the group. Grandma starts humming louder. Grandpa walks off the porch toward Danny, and Cocoa leaps out of the car, running to her brother. I go after her, telling Grandma I don't think she should run across the street by herself. A good excuse to be up close to Jay.

Grandpa doesn't yell or ask any questions. He just tells Danny and Ricky to get in the car. They get in, heads hanging low. I look at Jay. He is the only one who does not look ashamed. I need to start praying harder.

The whole way home Grandma is asking Danny and Ricky questions: What were you two thinking? Why did you lie to us? Ricky and Danny have no good answers. Grandpa looks through the rearview mirror, eyes of fire. "Well, I hope it was worth it."

Danny sighs. Grandpa always says, "Well, I hope it was worth it," before he gives out a punishment.

"I'm sorry, Pastor James," Ricky says. "I just want you to know that Danny didn't plan this. He didn't know my mother wouldn't be here."

Grandma stops humming. "But he knew it once he got there and he had a choice to leave or stay. Didn't you, Danny?"

"Yes, Grandma," Danny mumbles.

When we get home Grandma tells Danny and Ricky that they can't watch television or play any games. They are up in Danny's room pouting. Cocoa is content watching cartoons in the living room.

I pretend I have a lot to do in the bathroom so I can listen to Danny and Ricky through the wall. I sit down on the floor, ear to the wall and listen real close.

Ricky says, "Sorry I got you in trouble."

"Don't worry about it. My grandma's right. I could've left." They are quiet and I hear shifting, like one of them has gotten up from the bed. Danny keeps talking. "At least we made some good bread, though."

"Yeah. Dwayne hooked us up," Ricky says.

"What you gonna do with your half?"

"I'm saving it. I want to buy Maria something nice for Christmas."

My brother says, "Jay told me when we get tired of the small stuff to let him know and he'll tell Dwayne. He's got a few errands we can run for him."

"You thinkin' 'bout doing it?" Ricky asks.

"It's good money."

"Yeah," Ricky says. "With this kind of money, we'll never have to ask for anything."

AND FORGIVE US

· · · · · · · · · · ·

Serenity Evans
Mrs. Ross, 1st Period
Poetry Workshop

> **List Poem:** *a form of free-verse poetry.*
> *Write a List Poem about ten things you know.*

10 Things I Know

Even Jesus wept.
Everything tastes better when it's homemade.
Passing notes in class will get you in trouble.
Nobody likes to be made fun of.
True friends come back to you.

Saying "I'm sorry" is never easy.
A touch from a boy can set your soul on fire.
People who pass away
visit you in your dreams.
Sometimes doing the wrong thing
is the only way people know how to survive.
Death is a sneaky thief,
stealing life when you don't expect it.

It's the last day of school before winter break begins. Two weeks without coming to school! Grandma asked me if I wanted Maria to come over. I didn't tell her yes or no. I'm not sure right now where Maria and I stand. After school she is always running off to be with Ricky or Lisa. She told me that she is only hanging around Lisa because she feels bad being mean to someone who gave her such a nice gift.

We don't sit by each other anymore in English because Mrs. Ross made a seating chart. She says until the class is mature enough to handle sitting where we want, we'll all have assigned seats. I'm by Tyrone. He's quiet and really smart. He has the most silent reading points in the whole class. I'm second.

Mrs. Ross closes the door when the tardy bell rings. "Okay, class, I've got a lot to cover with you today." When she erases the dry-erase board, her hips wiggle from side to side. Most times she erases with her fingers and they turn blue, red, green, or whatever color marker she is using. I notice the hole in Mrs. Ross's stockings. It's huge and it's spreading. I know she must feel it. Tyrone taps me on the shoulder and gives me a note that Maria has passed up the line. Her note is in pink ink. It reads, "You should invite Mrs. Ross to church since she so holy!" I don't mean to laugh out loud, but I can't help it.

Mrs. Ross turns around. "Is something funny, Serenity?"

I can't stop laughing.

"Would you like to tell the class what's so funny?"

I laugh harder. "I'm sorry Mrs. Ross. I'm—sorry—I just—can't—stop—laughing."

"Well, maybe detention will help you get serious about learning. No recess for you," she says, glaring at me. I think she knows that I am laughing at her. She fixes her clothes, smoothing out the wrinkles and making sure the split in the back of her skirt is in the middle. I think of my grandpa asking me if it was worth it and I say to myself, *Yes. It's worth it to laugh and get in trouble if it means Maria and I are still friends. She passed the note to* me, *not Lisa.*

Mrs. Ross explains to us what our homework will be during winter break. The class is grumbling over the fact that we even have to do work when we are supposed to be on vacation. Mrs. Ross says, "You will work with a partner to create a report and presentation on one of the poets we've studied during our poetry workshop." While she explains and writes on the board how many pages the essay has to be, how long the presentation should be, and what it should cover, Tyrone taps me again.

Another note from Maria. "Want to be partners?"

I am so excited that things are getting back to normal that I don't even realize Mrs. Ross is standing right in front of me. "Is reading that more interesting than reading the board, Serenity?" Mrs. Ross takes the note right out of my hand and keeps telling the class about the presentation requirements. When people start choosing partners, she calls me up to her desk. She looks across the room, crumples Maria's note, and says, "Your partner will be Sommer." I could just scream I am so mad.

"Well, then, who am I going to be with?" Maria asks.

Mrs. Ross looks at the class. "Who doesn't have a partner yet?" Two boys and Lisa raise their hands. She puts the boys together and tells Maria, "You can be with Lisa."

When the bell rings, I exchange information with Sommer. The good thing is Sommer and I already know who we want to do our presentation on. Maya Angelou. I go into the hallway, stop at my locker, and walk outside to meet Danny.

"Serenity, wait up!" Maria is running behind me. There is no Lisa in sight. "Sorry I got you in trouble."

"It wasn't your fault. I'm the one who couldn't stop laughing."

"Yeah—that part was your fault." Maria smiles. Then she says, "Oh, and I meant to tell you, I like your hair that way." Maria runs her fingers through my braids. I'm wearing them down today.

"Thanks," I tell her. And I know this is Maria's way of saying sorry for everything else too. And I forgive her without her even really asking.

Instead of Maria and Ricky going off by themselves, they walk with the rest of us. Ever since Ricky and Danny's big lie, they have to go straight home after school. So we all walk slowly to make the time last. Maria and Ricky walk hand in hand and I am behind them between Danny and Jay. Danny and Ricky are getting off punishment just in time for winter break. They make plans for what they're going to do and then we all start talking about what we want for Christmas.

Maria says she wants clothes. She doesn't know that Ricky is getting her a really nice bracelet. He told me the last time he was over visiting Danny. I want another journal because mine is almost full and I want pens with all kinds of colored ink. I hate writing in only black or blue. "What do you want, Jay?" Maria asks.

"A kiss from Serenity." Everyone makes a big fuss over Jay saying this. Danny is laughing the hardest. Jay looks at me. "I'm serious," he whispers. I smile and keep walking like what he said didn't just make my heart skip.

When we get to Ricky's block, he and Maria leave the group. "See you guys later," they say.

Jay walks with me and Danny and once we are at my house, Danny goes inside. "See you two lovebirds later."

"Whatever!" I yell as the screen door slams shut. Danny starts making kissing noises and then he closes the door.

Jay asks, "You have Mrs. Ross for English, right?"

"Yeah."

"Who are you doing your report on?"

"Maya Angelou," I answer.

"I'm doing mine on Langston Hughes."

"Really?"

"You sound surprised."

"I just—I didn't know you even knew who any of the poets were. You're hardly in school." I sit down on the porch and Jay sits with me.

"I keep up though. I try to make up my work and I always bring a note to excuse my absence."

"From who?"

"My grandmother. She's sick. I take care of her. She's always in and out of the hospital or too sick to stay home by herself, so I stay with her. She's all I got." Jay tells me how he's never known his dad and his mom is on drugs. He tells me how she is in and out of his life. "I gotta hustle just to get clothes and food. And help pay for my grand-mother's prescriptions."

"I'm sorry," I say. And I am feeling real bad for judging Jay.

Jay tells me more about his grandmother and then he stands. "I should get out of here," he says. "Call me tonight," he says.

"Okay."

We hug.

When I get inside the house, Danny starts making kissing noises. "I'm telling," he says.

"Telling what?"

Danny gives me a look.

"We were just talking," I say.

"I don't care if you like Jay. But weren't you the same person who warned me about being his friend?" Danny goes into the kitchen and rummages through the cabinets until he finds a snack. He opens a bag of chips.

"I'm not running the streets with Jay. I don't steal from stores or sell weed."

"You're not perfect, Serenity!"

"I never said I was." All of a sudden we're arguing and yelling. "You need to act like you got some sense before you end up—"

"Like who?"

I don't say anything.

"Say it. Before I end up like who?"

I swallow everything I want to say.

Danny pours chips in a bowl. "I can take care of myself, Serenity. I don't need you worrying about me." He walks past me and leaves the kitchen.

"I don't mean to nag you," I say. "I'm sorry." But Danny is halfway up the stairs before I get the words out.

OUR DEBTS

· · · · · · · · · · ·

Serenity Evans
Mrs. Ross, 1st Period
Journal Entry

> "What happens to a dream deferred?"
> —Langston Hughes

Christmas is in two days. Being out of school has been so much fun. Pastor Mitchell planned activities for the youth during the day so that parents have a place to bring their children while they're at work. My favorite activity was going to Snow Bunny Lodge at Mt. Hood. We went sledding and right before we loaded back on the bus Ricky started a snowball fight—kids against adults. Pastor

Mitchell is fast! He barely got hit. Maria and I were soaking wet. Today there aren't any activities. Pastor Mitchell and his wife left to visit family up in Tacoma. Since there are no outings today, I've decided to work more on the poet study presentation. I am in my room getting dressed when my Grandma calls for me. "Serenity, Sommer is here!"

"Okay. I'm coming," I say. Maria and Lisa should be here soon. Sommer came up with the idea that just because we had to be with the partner Mrs. Ross assigned didn't mean we couldn't work as a group. So Lisa and Maria have been coming over to work on their poet, Sandra Cisneros, while Sommer and I work on Maya Angelou.

At first I wasn't too sure how I felt about having Lisa in my house. I told Ann about it and she said it might be a good chance for me to get to know Lisa. Maybe there was another side to her. And at least I'd get to be with Maria. What would it hurt? Ann asked me. So far, I have not seen many other sides of Lisa. She turns her nose up when my grandma offers her food, she bosses Sommer around, and I hear her telling Maria how their presentation is going to be the best because she's going to use a color printer for the presentation boards.

The only other side I've seen of Lisa is the side that gets all soft around the edges whenever Danny comes around. She starts to stutter and her light brown face turns red. Grandma notices, I think. So earlier today, before anyone came over, she asked Danny, "Don't you have some homework to work on while the girls are down-stairs?" He didn't, so she sent him over to the church to help Grandpa and Deacon Harris decorate the sanctuary for the Christmas program. Before he left, he told me to tell Lisa he said hi.

We work on our presentations and once Maria has her introduction paragraph written, she asks us all to listen. "Okay, tell me how this sounds," Maria says. She stands up, as if she's in class, and reads, "Sandra Cisneros is the only girl out of seven children. Her family lived in run-down apartments in Chicago's South Side while she was growing up." Maria squints at her paper. She takes her pencil, fixes a mistake, and keeps reading. "When she was a teenager, her family accomplished one of their dreams and bought a house. But Sandra Cisneros thought the new house was ugly and old." Maria sits down. "That's all I have so far, but next I'm going to write about how reading about Sandra Cisneros's life has taught me that sometimes, even when your dream comes true, it might not turn out like you thought it would," she says.

"I think it's good," Sommer says.

I nod. "Me too."

Just when Sommer and I are about to start the art on our poster board, Danny barges in the front door sob-bing and screaming, "Grandma! Grandma!" His shirt is covered in blood. "Grandma!"

My grandma runs out of her bedroom. "What, baby? What's the matter?"

"Grandma, I'm sorry. I'm sorry I didn't go straight to church and help Grandpa like you told me to."

"Danny, baby, what's wrong? What happened to you?"

Danny can barely catch his breath he's crying so hard. And even though I know he sees all of us—me, Maria, Sommer, and Lisa—he doesn't care that he is crying like a baby and that we can see him. He is shaking and he keeps looking behind him, like he is expecting someone to be there.

My grandma grabs him by his shoulders. "Danny—talk to me! What happened?"

"They killed Ricky," he says.

Maria throws her book on the table and runs over to Danny. "What?"

Danny tells Grandma the whole story. "I was going to go to church. I swear. But I went to Ricky's first. And—and we called—we called Jay's friend Dwayne to see if he had any work for us and he did. So we went to run his errand and then—then as we were walking back we saw that boy from school. The one we fought 'cause he was talking about me and Serenity. But he wasn't alone. He was with some older guys. One of them had a gun. They yelled at us, 'Try to fight him now.' But me and Ricky just walked away. We weren't trying to start trouble. But they followed us, driving real slow, and then—then the boy got out of the car and ran up on me. Ricky jumped in the middle to help me. Then the older one, he shot Ricky. Just shot him and told the boy to get back in the car. And they—they just drove off." Danny's chest is heaving up and down, his cheeks and lips are shaking, like he's been left outside for hours on the coldest winter day.

Maria's face is drenched in tears. Grandma calls for an ambulance and rushes with Danny to Ricky's house. She tells me to call my grandpa and to wait here. "Nobody leave," she tells us.

Maria doesn't listen. She follows them. "I want to see him. I want to see him!" She runs out of the house. I try to get her to stay. She thinks she's going to see Ricky as she knows him but I know that the moment someone dies, they don't look the same.

• • • • • • •

Restoration Baptist Church looks different whenever there are weddings or funerals. Today the altar is full of flowers and there is standing room only. Hundreds of people are here. Pastor Mitchell even came back early from his trip to say good-bye to Ricky. People are outside in the parking lot waiting to get one last look at Ricky.

Pastor McGee is standing at the pulpit hollering into the mike. "Don't worry about Ricky. He's in a better place!" He is dripping with sweat and even though he has a handkerchief in his hand, he doesn't use it. "Did you hear what I said? Ricky is in a better place!" The church says, "Amen," and the organist follows Pastor McGee's lead, like suspense music in movies. "That's why we are not sad today. This is not a funeral. This is a home going! We are not mourning. We are celebrating the life of dear Ricky."

I look at Ricky's mother. Tears have smeared her makeup. She doesn't look like she's celebrating. Pastor McGee continues to preach. "My dear sister, fear not, for you will see your son again." He steps out of the pulpit and walks over to the family. He grabs Ricky's mother's hand. "For the Bible says in Revelations 21 that when we get to heaven, 'God will wipe away all tears from our eyes; and there shall be no more death, neither sorrow, nor crying, neither shall there be any more pain: for the former things are passed away!'" He lets go of her hand and she collapses into the arms of her boyfriend.

"Oh yes, my sister, you will see your son again. And his body will be brand-new. It will not be marred with bullet wounds! It will be new . . . brand-new. And you will be new with him . . . worshipping God forever and ever. Yes, this is the promise to them that believe!" Pastor McGee walks back into the pulpit and lowers his sweaty palms like a conductor, ordering the organist to soften the music. He talks slower. "Young people, if you want to see Ricky again you've got to get your life right. If you want this joy I'm talking about—this joy you see in the faces of the saints, in the hope that we have in Christ Jesus, you must be born again."

Pastor McGee stops talking. He just stands in the

pulpit looking down at the flower-covered casket that is stretched in front of him. "You never know when death will come. And sometimes it comes and takes the one you least expect." He wipes his brow for the first time with the handkerchief in his hand. Pastor McGee looks sad for a moment. "Saints, we must not be angry or bitter. I say even to those young men who took his life, that there is love and grace and salvation for you."

The church says, "Amen."

Danny bends his body into itself, his face cupped in his hands. I put my hand on his back and rub it, but I know this is no comfort. I know that the images in Danny's head need more than my sympathy. I know that he will never forgive those boys. I know he will never forgive himself.

After Pastor McGee finishes preaching, two men in black suits walk to the front of the church. They slide the flowers that sit on the casket to the right side and lift the left section of the casket. Cries and sobs spill out of Ricky's family and some of them gasp, as if they didn't know he was in there. As if they thought he was just asleep.

Danny and I get in line behind Maria. We stand there for a long time. Maria is holding up the line. She is putting pictures in Ricky's casket and crying like a child throwing a tantrum. Someone escorts her out. When it is our turn to look, I just stare at the carpet and at the shiny wheels that hold the casket up. When I look back at Ricky's weeping mother I remember sitting in that same spot. I wonder if I ever will again. I also wonder why we have to wait till we get to heaven to have our tears wiped away.

I don't realize that Jay is at the funeral until we go outside. We are all waiting for the family to say their last good-byes to Ricky before they carry the casket out. Jay comes over to me and Danny. Danny barely looks at him. Jay says hello and the three of us stand there. Six men carry Ricky's body out. When it passes by us, Jay looks away. He isn't crying like Danny is, but he grabs my hand. Not like he's done before, when he's trying to be romantic. This time, he grabs my hand like he needs something to hold on to. Like he might fall if I don't hold him up. He is squeezing my hand tight, so tight I couldn't let go if I wanted to.

AS WE FORGIVE

· · · · · · · · · ·

Serenity Evans
Journal Entry

"Forgive one another."
—Colossians 3:13

Every time I wake up, I remember that Ricky is gone.
Each new day makes it more real. Grandpa says Danny
got a wake-up call. Ever since Ricky died, he's been paying close attention to Danny. He's started having men's
night on Fridays. Danny, Grandpa, and Ivan hang out in
the garage fixing cars and talking. Sometimes they go
to the movies or out to eat.

Today, Ivan and Erica are joining us for dinner. Grandma made gumbo. She calls us to the dining room and we all come to the table as fast as we can, our mouths watering, stomachs growling. This is the first day since Ricky's funeral that I am truly hungry and want to eat.

Danny is the first one to sit down at the table. Ivan taps him on his shoulder and tells him, "Let the ladies be seated first. Pull the chair out for your sister."

Danny does what Ivan tells him without grumbling.

Once we're all seated and eating, my grandma gets to telling stories about Ivan when he was our age. "You sure have come a long way." She laughs.

"You got that right," he says. "Remember when I skipped your class and forged my mom's signature on a note that said I'd been sick?"

"Yeah. I knew your mom didn't write it because you misspelled stomach flu," Grandma says.

Danny asks, "How did you spell it?"

Ivan shakes his head in embarrassment. "Instead of F-L-U, I wrote F-L-E-W." We all make fun of him. Erica is laughing the hardest. "Hey, I was only in the sixth grade. I wasn't the best speller."

Grandma adds, "You weren't the best liar either." She wipes the corners of her mouth with her napkin. "I could always tell when Ivan wasn't telling the truth because he'd start scratching his head."

"Good to know," Erica says.

Grandma and Ivan keep swapping stories about how mischievous Ivan was. I wonder if maybe years from now, Ivan and Erica will be remembering how Jay and Danny were and if they will be saying what good men they've turned out to be.

When I'm finished with my gumbo, Danny asks, "You want more or are you done?"

"I'm done," I tell him. He takes my bowl into the kitchen with his.

Even though Grandma made peach cobbler for dessert, we're all too stuffed to eat any right now. We go into the living room and flip channels until we all agree on what to watch. Grandpa is half asleep in his favorite chair and Grandma isn't really paying attention to the television. She's mostly reading the paper.

Erica whispers to Ivan, "We should get going. We have our appointment at the flower shop at nine o'clock in the morning."

"Nine o'clock?" Ivan isn't whispering. "I have to go to work. Why can't we go in the evening?"

"Baby, I told you about this last week."

"Erica, you did not tell me the appointment was at nine o'clock."

"Yes, I did."

Ivan and Erica go back and forth about this for a while. They are trying to whisper, but eventually they start talking loud and go into the kitchen, and the conversation stops being about the time of the appointment and starts being about other things.

I get knots in my stomach and my heart is doing somersaults. Grandma is just reading the paper as if she can't hear them arguing. "Aren't you going to stop them?" I ask Grandma.

"They're fine," Grandma says.

I listen. Back and forth they go until Ivan says, "I don't know. Maybe you did tell me."

"I can reschedule it if you want," Erica says.

And then they start talking about another time to go and Ivan tells Erica that he doesn't mind if she goes with one of her bridesmaids or Grandma. He trusts her. She has good taste.

My heart is still and the knots in my stomach unwrap themselves.

Ivan and Erica come out of the kitchen. "Sorry, guys. Prewedding quarrels," Erica says.

Grandma smiles. "Every couple has them."

And just like that it's over, and Erica and Ivan are watching TV with us again and our bellies have made room for Grandma's peach cobbler and we wake Grandpa and eat dessert together in the living room.

After Ivan and Erica leave, we all go to bed. I fall right to sleep, but then my dreams take me back to my old house, to the kitchen, to my momma and daddy arguing and fighting, to my momma's frozen eyes, the gunshot, and my daddy sitting in his car, dead. I wake up sweating and crying and I am afraid that if I go back to sleep, I'll dream again, so I get out of bed and go downstairs.

I sit on the sofa in the living room, wrapped in a throw blanket. I turn the TV on and turn the volume down real low. So low I can barely hear it. Nothing good is on anyway. Just long commercials about treadmills, diet pills, and acne creams.

The Bible on the coffee table is opened to the scripture Pastor McGee read at Ricky's funeral. Revelations 21. The scripture about waiting till we get to heaven for peace and for our tears to be wiped away. I keep seeing Ricky's mom. And my mom. And I keep thinking about all the tears I've been crying lately. And I want to throw the Bible on the floor, rip out its pages, and watch them burn in the fireplace. Why do I have to wait for peace? God is cruel.

Grandma comes out of her room and walks toward the bathroom. "Serenity, baby, is that you?"

"Yes."

"What's wrong?"

"I—I just." I can't tell her. I can't tell her how I don't understand why she keeps praying and going to church. I can't tell her that I want to forget every scripture I've ever memorized and take back every prayer I ever prayed because God isn't answering them anyway. My momma, my daddy, my friend all gone.

"Are you all right, baby?"

"I—" I can't say these things. Not to a woman who lives and walks by faith. I can retell Grandpa and Grandma's testimonies by heart. I can't tell them that I think God has forgotten about me. "I don't feel good," I say.

"Well, turn the television off and go get in bed, sweetheart." Grandma puts her hand on my forehead. "I hope you're not coming down with the flu." She takes her hand away.

I walk upstairs to my room, get in bed, and turn onto my stomach. I don't want to see heaven tonight.

· · · · · · ·

Sunday morning starts off like it always does. Sizzling bacon, scrambled eggs, and waffles waking my nose, telling me it's breakfast time. Telling me to hurry down before Danny eats it all. But I ignore the smells today and I plug my nose with willpower.

Grandma knocks on my door and when she comes in, I want to yell and say, *This is my room! Turn off the light! Leave me alone! I am not going to church today! I am never going back!* From now on I will spend my Sundays reading or watching TV, or writing in my journal. Anything but going to church.

"I'm not feeling any better," I tell Grandma.

"What hurts?" she asks.

"My stomach." And my heart.

Grandma leaves the room and comes back with a can of

ginger ale. "This should help." She puts a plastic bin by my bed in case I vomit. "I would stay but I have to sing today."

"It's okay, Grandma. I just want to sleep anyway."

"We'll come straight home after service," she promises. She leaves the room, closing the door behind her.

When I hear the car pull out of the garage, I get out of bed and listen to my music. I listen to the same song three times. I am so bored. Staying at home isn't as fun as I thought it would be. There's nothing on television on Sunday afternoons.

I decide to finish working on my presentation for English class. I haven't touched my half since before Ricky's funeral, and Sommer called yesterday asking when we would get together to glue everything on the poster board and practice.

I take the handouts Mrs. Ross gave us on Maya Angelou and underline the important parts. Mrs. Ross says that's a good note-taking skill. Underline the key points and use those to write an essay. I underline the facts that stick out most to me: Maya Angelou was born Marguerite Johnson in St. Louis, Missouri, on April 4, 1928. When she was three she was sent with her brother to live with their grandmother in Stamps, Arkansas. I underline how she's published over twelve books and how she has been in plays and movies and how she speaks not only English, but French, Spanish, Arabic, Italian, and Ghanaian Fante.

After I underline all that, I start to write the essay.

I work for a while, then decide to take a break. I decide to call Jay. He's the only person I know who's not in church right now.

Jay answers on the second ring. "Danny?"

"No, it's me. Serenity."

"You're not at church today?"

"I'm sick."

"Oh. Well, I hope you feel better."

"Thanks." I don't really have much to say to him. Guess I just wanted to hear his voice.

We talk for a few minutes and then Jay tells me he has to go.

"Okay," I say. "Talk to you later."

We hang up and I go back to writing my essay.

I'm on the second page when the doorbell rings. I go to the door and look through the peephole. Jay is here. He is holding a plastic grocery bag in his hand. I don't know what to do. I can't let him in. I can't let him see me like this. I am wearing sweats and a T-shirt and my hair is wrapped in a scarf. He rings the doorbell again. "Just a minute!" I take off my scarf and shake my braids to make my hair fall into place.

When I open the door Jay steps in and gives me a hug. "Sorry you're not feelin' well." He holds the bag out to me. "I got you some orange juice from the corner store."

"Thank you." I take the juice into the kitchen and pour a glass. "You want some?"

"No. It's for you," Jay says. He sits at the dining room table. "You look good for a sick girl."

I smile.

Jay looks at the pile of papers and books on the dining room table. "Man, even when you're sick you do homework?" He picks up my report and starts reading it.

"What do you think?" I ask.

"Well," Jay says. He rereads the paper, and when he puts it back on the table, he says, "It's all right."

"All right?" All of my words are spelled correctly, I have made sure all my facts are from the class handouts, I have quotes, and I even talked about what some of her poems mean to me. "What do you mean it's all right?"

"You did good. I would just add more about her. Not just her work," Jay says. Who does Jay think he is? He barely comes to class and he's telling me how to write a report. He picks up the class handouts Mrs. Ross gave us on Maya Angelou's life. "Look, you don't even talk about the good stuff."

He points to the third paragraph on the handout and starts reading, "When Maya Angelou was seven, she moved back with her mother. A few months later, her mother's boyfriend sexually abused her. When Maya told what happened, her uncles beat the man to death. She became mute for almost six years, believing that the power of her words led to someone's death." Jay clears his throat and then shows me the handout, like he wants me to know he's not making it up.

He keeps reading out loud and I read along with him. "After returning to live with her grandmother, she found a close friend and teacher who helped her rediscover her voice."

I read the last line out loud with him. "She began to speak again in her early teens."

"Why didn't you put any of this in your report?"

I shrug my shoulders.

"I mean, I like her poems but I like them more 'cause she's writing about what she's been through. People probably thought she wasn't gonna be anything, but look who she became."

I take my pen and underline the paragraph we just read. "You're right," I say. "Writing about her awards and the languages she speaks is kind of dull." I pick my essay back up and look it over. "I'll add this stuff. Tell how she took all that pain and made it into something."

I look at the picture of Maya Angelou that's on the bottom of my handout. She is smiling and there is no sadness in her eyes. Jay says, "That's why I don't let stuff get me down. Everybody got bad stuff in their life, you know? Don't mean it's always gonna be that way," he says. Then he scoots back his chair. "I better go. I don't want you to get in trouble. I know your grandparents don't like me."

"They like you. Who told you that, Danny?"

"No. I just know."

"That's not true. They're just strict. But they like you."

"Do you?"

I answer him before thinking and boldness I have never felt before comes over me. I lean in close to Jay and say, "Yes, I like you a lot." And then I kiss him. Maria is right, kissing is better than the best meal you've ever had. And Jay's lips are perfectly kissable.

When my lips stop kissing Jay's, he stands up and walks to the door. He smiles at me and kisses me once more, a soft peck on the lips. "I'll see you later. Hope you feel better."

"Bye." I close the door. I feel better. Much better.

Jay's only been gone for five minutes when Grandpa's car pulls in the driveway. I pray they didn't see him walking from the house. I run to my room and get into bed. Grandma calls up to me, "Serenity, we're home!" I hear her tell Danny to come check on me.

Danny knocks on my door. I tell him to come in. "You feelin' better?"

"Yeah."

Danny stands there looking at me.

"What?"

"Nothing." Danny is still standing there, looking at me.

"What do you want?"

"Serenity, I'm sorry." Danny looks like he wants to say

more. Like he wants to apologize for every single thing he's ever done to make me mad or frustrated.

I think about the things I've done too. How I didn't have to yell, or be bossy. "I'm sorry, too, Danny," I say.

We don't say anything for a while. Danny walks over and sits on my bed. He asks, "Are you really sick?"

"No," I tell him.

"I didn't think so."

"Don't tell."

"I won't," he promises. Then Danny, the expert on getting in and out of trouble, says, "Just remember that if you were too sick to go church, you can't eat dinner tonight. You should just ask for soup or something."

"Good point."

"I'll put some real food aside for you and bring it upstairs, okay?"

"All right," I say and even though I am not really sick, I feel like lying down. I feel tired and I don't have energy to do anything. I stay under the covers and look up at my ceiling, wondering if Ricky has seen my momma yet. If either of them knows how much we miss them.

I've been asleep for an hour when Grandma comes in my room carrying a tray with a bowl of soup and a pack of saltine crackers for me. "Serenity, baby, you need to eat something."

I sit up, groggy, and take the tray. I take a few bites while she is standing there, but when she leaves, I put it to the side. I don't want to get full. I'm saving room for the real food that Danny's bringing. It feels like me and Danny are becoming brother and sister again, like before. Like we're on the same team.

OUR DEBTORS

· · · · · · · · · · ·

Serenity Evans
Mrs. Ross, 1st Period
Poetry Workshop

Write about how you spent your spring break.

Spring cleaning.
Rummaging through boxes in the basement.
Giving away clothes, dishes, old things
not used anymore.
Grandma says it's good to go through
your stuff every now and then.
Reminds you how good God's been.
All the blessings He's given you.

So many, you got enough to give away.
There's a box in the corner of the basement.
It has been closed since I moved here.
Always.
I open it today.
Spring cleaning day.
And I see my momma's heels.
And I am sad because all she left me was a
pair of shoes.

It's March and Mrs. Ross keeps saying that she can't believe how time is flying. "You graduate in just a few months. It's time to start thinking about where you want to go next year." I am excited about high school. Maria and I have already decided—we are going to Northside High.

I hope Jay is going too. I haven't seen him lately so I haven't been able to ask. I don't talk a whole lot about me and Jay to Maria. I know she is happy for me but I know seeing me with Jay makes her miss Ricky even more, so I try not to tell her much. Like I didn't tell her about the journal he gave me on Valentine's Day. Instead, we talk about going to high school and we make plans for what electives we're going to register for. Maria, of course, wants to sing in the choir. I thought about taking art, but Mrs. Ross thinks I should take the after-school creative writing class.

Mrs. Ross says she is proud of us and excited. "You all will have to come back and visit me when you go to high school. Don't forget about us." Mrs. Ross tells us all the time how much she is going to miss us. Some of my other teachers say it too. But I think Mr. Harvey is ready for us to go and hopes to never, ever see us again.

When we get to Mr. Harvey's class he is already in a bad mood because of something that happened with the class before us. So when he catches me and Maria passing notes, he explodes. "Maria, I want you to come sit over here!" Mr. Harvey yells and pulls out the chair beside Bobby.

"Mr. Harvey, I will sit anywhere else but there. Please," Maria says.

"You need to learn how to follow instructions. This is not up for discussion." The class is silent, waiting to see what Maria is going to do.

"But, Mr. Harvey, please. Can't I sit somewhere else?"

"Maria, I'm not asking again."

Mr. Harvey thinks Maria is just being her regular stubborn self, but Bobby is the cousin of that boy who killed Ricky. "I'll switch," I tell Mr. Harvey, but that is not good enough.

"Thank you, Serenity, but I asked Maria." He walks up to Maria and looks in her eyes. "Since you can't follow instructions, you can't be in class." Mr. Harvey writes a referral for Maria and sends her to the office. Maria starts cursing and yelling. She throws the referral back at him and walks out of the room. "Young lady! Young lady, where do you think you're going?" Mr. Harvey is yelling down the hall. He slams the door and makes us read silently from our books for the rest of the period.

While we read, he picks up the phone and calls the main office. "Maria Mosley just walked out of class. I've written her a referral and I do not want her back in this class without a parent conference."

I look over at Bobby. He looks sad. I'm sure he knows why she didn't want to sit by him. When the bell rings, I run out of class. I try to find Maria. I go to both our lockers, to the choir room, and to the bathroom stalls. I can't find her. Then I see Maria and Isabel walking out of the office. Isabel doesn't even smile at me. She just grabs Maria's hand and says, "When we get home I want you to pack your stuff. I've had enough."

When school lets out I meet Danny in our usual spot. Jay is there, even though he wasn't in school. He hugs me, but I let go quicker than either of us expect. "Danny, if Grandma asks, I'm at Maria's. I have to go check on her," I tell him.

"Hold up," Danny says. "I'll come with you."

"It's okay. Go with Jay. That's fine. I'll see you at the house."

"But—" Danny says.

"Really, Danny, it's okay."

Jay says, "Yeah man, I got somethin' for us to do anyway."

I start to walk away. I hear Danny telling Jay that he needs to get home and start his homework so he can't go. I think whatever Ivan is saying to Danny is sinking in. And I feel weird, liking and hugging and kissing the boy that everyone is shooing away.

I know I shouldn't like Jay. I mean—liking him as a friend is fine, but I know that sneaking around with him is wrong. Everyone always tells girls not to like boys like him but they never tell us how not to.

When I get to Maria's, she is sitting on the porch crying. I sit next to her. "I hate her, Serenity. I really do."

"Don't say that."

"She's making me stay with my dad." Maria wipes her tears away, but more come as soon as she talks again.

"Did you explain to your mom what happened? Did you tell her why you didn't want to sit by Bobby?"

"She doesn't care. She said it doesn't matter. I should respect adults even if I disagree." Maria sniffs long and hard. "She said I need to get over Ricky. That I can't keep blaming my attitude on him." Maria stops talking. She stares at the ground at the line of ants crawling out of a tiny hole. "She's such a hypocrite. Talkin' 'bout how I've changed. How I let my relationship with Ricky take over me. Like she's not doing that. Talkin' 'bout she needs a break. She just wants to spend time with that ugly boyfriend of hers." Maria stops crying and wipes her wet hands on her jeans. "I should call my grandmother and have her send for me early. I want to go to Mexico now. I don't want to wait till summer."

I whisper, "Maria, why don't you just tell your mom why you don't want to stay with your dad?"

"I can't, Serenity. I can't."

"Well, do you want me to tell my grandma? I know she'll help you," I say.

"Serenity, no. You promised."

Isabel comes to the door. She talks through the screen. "Your father will be here soon. Come get your bags."

Maria gets up and walks in the house. I follow her to her bedroom and help her carry her bags. By the time we get outside, Maria's father is here. His car is parked outside the house, windows down. "You been giving your mother trouble, huh?" he says.

Maria ignores him and takes her bags to the back of the car. He pops the trunk. "Good luck with her," Isabel says. Then she digs in her pockets and pulls out money. I see her counting the bills—five ones, a five, and a twenty. "Maria, come here."

Maria slams the trunk and walks back up on the porch. "Here." Isabel hands her the money. "It's all I got."

Maria snatches it and walks back to the car. I follow her and before she gets in, I give her the biggest hug I can. I whisper in her ear, "Call me tonight, so I know you're okay."

Maria gets in the car. Her father starts the engine

and they drive away. I am standing on the sidewalk look-ing back at Maria's house. Isabel is on the porch watching the car drive away and I am thinking, it's not too late to stop them. But right when I think to say it, Isabel's boyfriend walks out, with his big belly, and says, "Is she gone yet?"

"Yeah. She just left."

Miguel takes her hand. "Good, now we can have some peace and quiet around here." They go inside the house and close the door.

I'm feeling real mad right now. Mad at every mother I know. I'm thinking about my momma leaving nothing for me, except a pair of shoes, nightmares, and secrets. I'm thinking about Maria and how her momma sent her on her way, giving her thirty dollars, and how Jay's momma never gave him anything. I'm thinking how not even Maya Angelou's momma could give her safety. I'm think-ing parents owe their children something more.

AND LEAD US NOT INTO TEMPTATION

. . . .

Serenity Evans
Mrs. Ross, 1st Period
Poetry Workshop

Haiku Formula: *3 lines of poetry, arranged in lines of 5, 7, and 5 syllables.*

Write a haiku about spring.

Springtime

Flowers are blooming.
Leaves have returned to their trees.
Winter left for good.

I've been able to get out of church for the past two Sundays. Jay comes over and we watch television and kiss and play cards and kiss and do homework and kiss. But I can't keep pretending to be sick, so we decide to skip school today so we can go to the park.

"I'm not going to be in class after lunch," I tell Maria on our way to my locker.

"Okay," she says, not even asking why. Maria looks like all the life is out of her. Like she doesn't care about anything or anyone. She's been quiet, and when I asked her if she wanted to talk to my grandparents, she said, "About what?"

Why do women and girls keep such horrible secrets?

The bell rings at the end of lunch and I just leave. I walk out of school like I'm not doing anything wrong. When I get to the park Jay is waiting for me at the swings. He's not swinging, just lightly swaying from side to side. His feet brush across the top of the dirt, making dust rise.

We sit for a while on the swings and then Jay tells me he has something to say. "So tell me," I say. And he leans in close to me and kisses my lips. The wind blows and I can feel how cold the tip of his nose is. I can hear the cars driving past, but I know they cannot see us because of the tall trees.

Jay gets up from off the swing. We walk through the fallen cherry blossoms onto a pathway that winds through the park. "I have something for you," Jay tells me.

"What?"

"It's a surprise." Jay walks me to the bus stop.

"Where are we going?"

"You'll see."

"I have to be back before school is out."

"You will be." Jay lets me on the bus first. We ride for five stops and get off at the mall.

"Here." Jay hands me a stack of gift cards.

At first I think, I can't take these. I think about how I told Danny this was so wrong. But I guess it doesn't matter now. If there's not a God who answers my prayers, there's not a God who'll punish me. He's not paying attention to anything I do.

When we get in the mall, I get all nervous. I feel like everyone knows that I don't belong here. That I have no money for clothes and shoes and jewelry. The first store we go into I only try on three things. The card has one hundred dollars on it and I am scared that it won't work when I hand it to the cashier, but it does. And so does the next one. And the next one. I have jeans, dresses, shoes, bracelets, earrings.

"We should take this stuff to your house before we go back to school," Jay says. He has it all figured out, like he planned this. He takes his cell phone out and calls someone. We wait outside, two bags in my hand, three in his. A black car pulls up to the curb. "Here's Dwayne." Jay lets me get in the car and he gets in after me. Some girl with high, stiff hair is sitting in the front.

"Thanks, man." Jay and Dwayne shake. "This is Serenity."

"Hey, shorty. Where am I taking you?"

"This is Danny's sister. We're going to his house."

Dwayne starts driving and I get to thinking, how does he know where we live? Dwayne gets to our house quick because he drives fast and takes only the back streets so we miss all the lights. His music is so loud, the bass vibrates inside my chest and shakes the windows.

"Here you go," Dwayne says as he pulls up to my house. "I'll wait out here."

Jay gets out of the car and helps me bring my bags inside. I stuff everything in my closet for now and rush back downstairs so I can get back to school to meet Danny at the flagpole so Grandma can take us to our counseling appointment.

When we get back in the car, Dwayne and the stiff-haired girl are smoking. I am so scared the smell will get in my clothes, but I have to ride with him. If I take the bus, I'll be late for sure. When we get a block away from Rose City Academy, Jay taps Dwayne on his shoulder. "You can drop us off here."

"All right." Dwayne pulls over. "Take care, shorty. Tell your brother to come through when he gets a minute."

I say, "Thanks for the ride." I get out of the car. Jay is right behind me. We make it to the flagpole ten minutes before the dismissal bell rings. I hug Jay good-bye and he leaves before Danny or Maria come out. By the time Danny gets to the flagpole, Grandma has pulled up. We walk to the car, get in, and go to see Ann and Gloria. Grandma doesn't suspect a thing.

BUT DELIVER US FROM EVIL

· · · · · · · · · · ·

Serenity Evans
Mrs. Ross, 1st Period
Poetry Workshop

*"My great hope is to laugh
as much as I cry."*
—Maya Angelou

I step into the counseling center and send Danny to Gloria. "I have to use the bathroom. Don't wait for me," I say. Danny gets on the elevator. Instead of going to the restroom, I walk around the center, then cross the sky bridge and enter the hospital. I refuse to see Ann today.

All she is going to do is make me cry and think and talk. I just want to walk right now.

I look on the directory and find the floor that has the cafeteria. I go into my change purse and get coins for the vending machine. I have enough for two bags of chips and a candy bar. When I finish eating, I walk around more. There are all sorts of people here. Some look happy, others worried, a few relieved. I walk to the emergency waiting room. When you look at some of the patients that are waiting, you can tell immediately what's wrong with them.

A man is sitting with his hand wrapped in a torn T-shirt. Blood is seeping through and he's holding it, rocking back and forth. There's a little kid bent over in a woman's lap. He is holding his stomach and crying. But the woman across from them looks fine. She is sitting in the seat like nothing is wrong and I think maybe she is waiting for someone, but then a nurse calls her name and I realize she is a patient.

I look at the clock. Grandma will be here soon. I walk back across the sky bridge and meet Danny in the lobby and we get in the car. When we get home, I go straight upstairs. Everything I've done today is weighing on me and I'm starting to feel like that woman in the hospital. No one can tell by looking at me, but there's something wrong on the inside.

Danny knocks on my door.

"Yes?"

"You got something in the mail. Grandpa told me to give it to you."

"Come in."

Danny hands me an envelope from the church. It's my Rites of Passage confirmation letter. The letter is congratulating me. I have completed my community service hours and my statement of faith has been reviewed. I will be passed at the ceremony in May. At the bottom of the letter it tells me that I need to reply and tell Mrs. Mitchell what scripture I will be reciting. I look at the bags of clothes in my closet and I put the envelope in the drawer of my desk. I don't even know if I want to go through with the ceremony anymore.

I'm not sure how Grandma makes it up the stairs without me hearing the floor creak, but here she is at my door. She doesn't knock; she just barges in. "Serenity, I just got off the phone with Ann." Grandma's eyes are sharp knives. I look away. "Why didn't you go to your session?" she asks. I'm thinking, maybe if I sit here long enough without saying anything, she will just punish me and we won't even have to talk about it. "Do you hear me? I asked you a question." Grandma closes my bedroom door, sits down on my bed, and asks me again. "Why didn't you go to your session today?"

"I don't want to talk to Ann anymore."

"Why not?"

"There's no point," I answer.

"What do you mean there's no point?" Grandma starts fussing at me. She goes on and on about Ann being a person and how it's not fair to just leave her sitting in an office waiting for me. She has feelings too. She fusses and fusses and fusses. "I just can't believe you'd do something like this. What were you thinking? Why would you—?"

"You want to know what I'm thinking? I'm thinking that talking to Ann is stupid and so is talking to God. Neither of them really cares about me. They just like to see me cry!" I can't stop the words from coming out now. "I don't ever want to go back to see Ann and I'm never going back to church again!"

I expect Grandma to hush me, but instead she just lets me talk. She lets me scream and yell about how unfair it is that I don't have a mother when I loved her so much and how Ricky died when, really, he was doing the right thing by sticking up for a friend. I tell Grandma that I am so mad, so angry that every time things start looking good they go bad. "It's not fair, Grandma. It's not fair." My eyes are so full of hot tears, I can barely see.

Grandma holds me and wipes my tears away with her plump hands, and now I can see that she is crying with me. "Serenity, baby. Who told you life was going to be fair?"

"Well, what's the point? What's the point of going to church and praying and doing right if nothing good is going to happen to you?"

"Baby, if you try to tally it up like that—you'll never

have peace or joy. You don't get rewarded right away for good deeds. And every time something bad happens doesn't mean God is out to get you." Grandma rubs my back and I cry softer and softer, and peace comes over me like at the end of a rainstorm.

Grandma looks me in my eyes and says, "Now I know you haven't baked in the kitchen for a while, but you do remember the main ingredients for a cake, don't you?"

I really don't feel like talking about her cookbook right now, but I say yes.

"And what are they?"

I sit back against my pillow and face Grandma. "Well, you need eggs, flour, and oil," I tell her.

"Right," Grandma says. "Now, tell me, would you ever eat a raw egg?"

"No, Grandma." I have no idea why she is asking me this.

"Would you take a spoon and eat spoonfuls of flour? Or drink a cup of oil?"

I am grossed out just thinking about it. "Grandma, that's nasty."

"Exactly. Those things don't taste good by themselves, do they?"

"No."

"But what happens when you mix all those ingredients together and bake it in the oven?"

"It tastes good," I answer.

Grandma smiles. "Real good if I'm baking it." Then she takes my hands. "Serenity, baby, it's the same way with life. The deaths of loved ones, friends hurting your feelings. There are all kinds of things that happen in life that don't feel good. They're just downright awful, but I know from experience that all those hard, hurtful things get combined with the good, joyful things and somehow the good outweighs the bad." Grandma shifts her weight and makes herself more comfortable on my bed. "You know how many times I've cried in my life? So many I can't count." Grandma smiles. "But guess what? I can't count the laughs either. I've had plenty of both," Grandma says. "It's been a tough year, Serenity, baby. I know. But it won't always hurt this bad."

Grandma lets go of my hands. "The next time you look at a cake with all that pretty frosting I want you to think about what it took to get it to look that good." She makes eye contact with me. "It's the same with life. You never know what not-so-sweet things have happened in someone's life—even the life you think is perfect. Do you understand what I'm saying?"

"Yes."

Grandma stands up and walks to the door. "Now, I'm not going to make you talk to Ann, but if you don't want to go back, you need to let me know so I can cancel it. Do you need to think about it before you make your final decision?"

"Yes," I tell her.

"Okay. We'll talk about it more tomorrow." Grandma says good night and closes my door.

I change my clothes and get into bed. I can hardly sleep thinking about what Grandma said. I know my momma isn't with me but right now it feels like she is. I hear her telling me, "I told you so." And she did. When I was younger, Momma read me bedtime stories. I always wanted her to skip to the end so I could know what would happen. Especially if there was a scary scene. I wanted to make sure that the characters would be okay. Momma would say, "You can't truly enjoy a happy ending if you skip through all the bad parts."

FOR THINE IS THE KINGDOM

· · · · · · · · · ·

Serenity Evans
Mrs. Ross, 1st Period
Poetry Workshop

"A bird doesn't sing because it has an
answer, it sings because it has a song."
—Maya Angelou

Grandma and Erica are in the kitchen at the banquet
hall talking about how time is flying. "April done rolled
around here quick," Grandma says. "I can't believe your
wedding is tomorrow." Grandpa has been teasing
Grandma that she's more excited about Erica's wedding
than she was about her own.

The banquet hall is beautiful. We decorated all night while the wedding party rehearsed for tomorrow's ceremony. Now that the rehearsal is over, we are having dinner to celebrate and so our family can spend time with Ivan's family.

Grandma's cooked a feast. I actually miss being in the kitchen, preparing the food and helping watch it. I asked Grandma if she needed any help, but by the time I asked, all the cooking was done. "But you can help me bring it out," she says. "Here, take these trays out to the table, please." Grandma points to the cheese, fruit, and vegetable trays she assembled. I take them out one at a time.

There are so many people here. Family from both sides and people who are in the wedding are lined up at the tables to fix their plates. I see faces that I do not recognize and some faces that have changed—more wrinkles, less hair.

The banquet hall is full of chatter and laughter and all kinds of noise. Babies are crying, music is playing. The gray-haired women sit at one table, reminding each other of how things used to be. Young girls sit across from them, at another table, talking about what they want to be.

Before we eat Grandpa says a prayer and Ivan's father gives a toast. People go back for seconds and thirds. I am sitting with my cousins Michael and Brian. Danny has been hanging out with them when he's not with Ivan. We are eating and talking when Erica comes over to the table. "I ate too much," she says. "I need to go walk some of this off." Erica rubs her stomach. "You want to come with me?"

"Okay." I throw my paper plate in the garbage and follow Erica to the deck that wraps around the building.

As we walk out on the deck, the voices from inside fade and all I can hear is the calming water under us tickling and teasing the rocks by coming to the shore and going back again.

After we walk around for a while, Erica sits down on a bench. I sit beside her. She takes her sandals off and frees her manicured toes.

"So what are you thinking about?" Erica asks.

"My momma."

"I've been thinking of her a lot, too," Erica tells me.

"She would have loved all of this. She would have been so happy for you and I know she'd be in the kitchen right now with Grandma cooking and baking."

I can almost hear my momma's laugh, see her walking this path with me. Sometimes she just shows up in my mind and it's like I feel her presence here, feel her right next to me.

"I miss her so much," I say. "Sometimes I feel like it's all my fault."

"Serenity, why? Why would you ever think that?"

"Because if I would have told what my dad was doing, how he was abusing her—maybe she could've gotten help."

"Oh, Serenity, that's such a big burden for you to carry." Erica scoots in real close to me. "Lots of people knew about your mom. I know she thought she was keeping it from us, but we knew."

"Really?"

"Well, we weren't positive, but we definitely suspected it. My mom, Grandma, Uncle Brian, me—we all tried to talk your mom into leaving your dad." Erica looks sad and I feel bad that she's talking about this the day before her wedding. "I think we all feel responsible. Like maybe we didn't try hard enough. We believed her lies too, I guess. She said she was okay and we believed her. But we all knew something wasn't right."

Erica takes a breath. "I think we expected her to come to us for help when she was ready. But some people are never ready. Sometimes they need someone to help them take the first step."

We sit for a moment, just taking in Portland's sun. My momma loved sitting outside. In the summer we would go to Waterfront Park and walk to the edge of the dock and just sit and talk. Just like this. I think about how I love to do this, just like my momma did. How I love to cook, just like my momma did. And I ask Erica, "Do you think children become their parents?"

Erica thinks for a moment before answering and then

says, "You don't have to be just like your parents. You can make different choices." Above our heads a flock of birds rest in a tree singing, chirping, and talking to each other. The sky is changing colors and it's getting chilly now that the sun is fading. Erica puts on her sandals and stands.

We walk back to the reception hall. And I just have to say one more thing before we go in. I stop on the deck and lean against the banister. Couples from the banquet have come out and are walking hand in hand. "Erica, you know how you said some people need someone to help them take the first step?"

"Uh-huh."

"What if I have a secret about someone who needs help taking the first step to get out of a bad situation?"

Erica says, "Serenity, you can't keep carrying everyone's burdens."

I look out at the water. Now that it's getting dark, the water looks like a bottle of black ink spilled on the ground.

"Is there something you need to tell me?" Erica asks.

I don't say anything.

"Serenity—"

"I'm not supposed to say anything," I tell Erica. "But I can't keep it in anymore. If something happens to Maria, I don't know what I'd do."

"What's going on with Maria?"

I tell Erica about Maria's dad. I know Maria is going to hate me for this, but I also feel like I kept my promise.

I swore I wouldn't tell my *grandparents*. I didn't say anything about my cousin.

Erica tells me, "I'll figure something out." And we come up with all kinds of options for Maria.

"She's going to be all right, Serenity," Erica says.

I hope so.

We walk back to the banquet hall. Voices circle around the room. Grandma's laugh is the loudest. She is laughing at Natasha, my three-year-old cousin. The family is circled around Natasha and she is in the middle dancing to the music, performing for everyone. Soon everyone starts dancing. My uncle tries to show off his dance moves. His children look embarrassed, but I think it's funny. I see Danny sitting next to Ivan, laughing hard and having a good time.

Grandma leaves the dance floor. "I need you again," she tells me. I follow her to the kitchen. It's time for the cake. She carefully places it in my hands and walks behind me, carrying extra jugs of punch. The cake is so pretty. It's Erica's favorite. A lemon cake with cream cheese frosting. It has Erica's and Ivan's names on it and there are flowers made out of frosting on the corner.

One of Ivan's aunts cuts the cake in squares. She gives me a big, big piece. "That's for helping," she says. I take a bite. "How does it taste?"

"Good," I tell her. And I think of Grandma and what she told me about cake. "Real good."

AND THE POWER
· · · · · · · · · ·

Serenity Evans
Mrs. Ross, 1st Period
Poetry Workshop

"I rise."
—Maya Angelou

I've asked Maria to come over after school. She has no idea what's about to happen, and I feel bad—like I'm setting her up—but I know that if I told her that her mom was waiting at my house, she wouldn't come.

As soon as we step on my block, Maria spots her mother's car. And Erica's. "Serenity, what's going on? What did you do? What did you do?" She stops walking.

I take a deep breath. "Maria, Erica said you could stay with her if you needed to." I say it real fast. It wasn't the plan to just blurt it out like that, but I don't know how else to say it.

Maria looks angry. Angry and confused. "Why would Erica say that?"

I answer, "Because I told her about your dad."

"Serenity—"

"Maria, listen to me!" I yell. "I couldn't let him hurt you and not say anything." I don't know where this new courage comes from. Maria doesn't either. She is quiet for a change and lets me do the talking. "Wouldn't you have done the same for me? If I was in trouble and needed help, wouldn't you have helped me?"

Maria's face is red.

"Your mom doesn't know yet. She just knows that you need to talk with her. Erica and my grandma are just there to support you, to help you."

Maria starts to walk away.

I grab her hand. "Let me help you. Please," I say. "Your dad shouldn't get away with this. And if your mom doesn't believe you, then you can stay with us or with Erica. But I'm not going to pretend like everything is fine and keep up this lie. You need to get out of your dad's house."

We walk to my house. I unlock the door and we step in. Erica, Grandma, and Isabel are sitting in the living room. Maria takes my hand. We sit down. I hold her hand while she tells her mother everything.

There are tears; there are apologies. And, thank God, there are promises made. Isabel holds Maria in her arms and says, "I wish you would have told me sooner. I'll never let him touch you again."

Grandma asks us to go to my room while the adults talk. When we get upstairs, Maria bursts into more tears.

"Don't cry, Maria," I say.

"These are good tears," she tells me. She's smiling and crying. "I can't believe you did this for me."

"I'd do anything for you," I tell Maria.

I did it for my momma too.

· · · · · · ·

I step into Ann's office feeling a little nervous. Grandma and I decided that it would be okay for me to take a break, so I haven't been to see her for the past two weeks.

"Anything you want to talk about?" Ann asks.

"I'm sorry about skipping out on you," I say.

"I understand. Sometimes it's just too much, huh?"

"Yeah," I say. "And I didn't want to talk about what I'd done."

"Do you want to talk about it now?"

I tell Ann about skipping school and going shopping with Jay. "But once I got home, it didn't feel good having those clothes. It still doesn't."

"Why not?"

"I feel guilty. I got the letter in the mail about the

Rites of Passage ceremony and I just feel bad. Like a hypocrite. I don't even need new clothes."

Ann asks, "How else do you feel?"

"Like my mom," I say. "I feel how she must've felt the day she died." Without even trying to, I remember every detail about the day my father came home early. "My momma was happy because the mail came. Every day for about two weeks my momma would get all excited when she saw the postman putting mail in our box. She'd run to see if that special envelope had come," I tell Ann.

Ann sits back and listens and I tell her everything I remember.

"One day Momma and I went to the library. She was typing something. I was reading a book the librarian picked out for me. Momma finished what she had been typing, printed it, and we went to the post office to mail it. Momma said to me, 'Serenity, can you keep a secret?'

"I told her I could. So Momma told me she was going to start taking classes at the culinary school downtown."

"Why was this a secret?"

"Because my daddy thought it was a waste of time and money to take classes on how to cook. But Momma wanted to enroll in a restaurant management program," I explain. "It wasn't just about cooking; it was so she could learn how to own a restaurant."

"I see," Ann says.

"My momma came up with a plan. She told me about

money that schools give to people who want to come to their school—they're called scholarships. Momma told me to keep it a secret, just in case she didn't get it. She didn't want to get my daddy upset for no reason. And she didn't want to get my grandparents' hopes up if she didn't get accepted."

I stop to catch my breath because I realize I am talking really fast. "Momma was so excited when she saw that envelope. She couldn't even open it. She handed it to me. I remember looking at the big envelope. Momma was rushing me, telling me to hurry and see what it said. I opened it and pulled out the first sheet of paper."

Ann looks interested to hear the rest and I am enjoying telling her. So far we have mostly talked about sad things with my momma. I am glad I am remembering more of the good. I tell Ann how I read the letter out loud to my momma. "Dear Mrs. Evans, we are pleased to inform you that you have been accepted into the Restaurant Management Program at Willamette Culinary Institute."

I remember Momma jumping out of her seat. She hugged me so hard and tight, squeezing all of me in her arms. She snatched the letter out of my hand and finished reading it to herself. "Serenity, oh, Serenity, do you know what this means? This means I'm going to own my restaurant one day!" She hugged me again and reread the letter. "A full-tuition scholarship! They're paying for everything!" she said.

I tell Ann how we turned on music and danced around the living room.

"Is that what the dinner was for?" Ann asks. "To celebrate?"

"Yes. Momma took me and Danny to the store and we filled the cart with everything she would need to make Daddy's favorite meal. We were all so happy. So excited that Momma's dream was going to come true. But then Daddy came home early and before Momma had a chance to sit down with him and explain it all, he saw the letter sitting on the counter."

I scoot back on the sofa and rest my back against one of the pillows. For the first time I am completely relaxed in Ann's office and I am not crying. "My daddy threw a wad of money on the table and said no matter what degree she had she'd never make that much money in one day."

I stop talking and look at Ann. "You know what happened after that," I say. "But before that, before my daddy walked in the kitchen, before he ruined her dream, my momma was the happiest I had ever seen her."

I exhale.

All the secrets are out.

• • • • • • •

Talking to Ann dug up memories I buried when my momma died. I remember my momma trying to teach me to ice skate and how she fell more times than I did. I remember her singing off-key to the radio when we drove to the store or the mall or school. I remember her telling me how education is important, and every day when I came home from school, she'd make me tell her one new thing I learned. I fall asleep looking at the stars on my ceiling and for each one I count, I think of something about my momma. I fall asleep and my dreams are sweet because my momma is there with me.

The next day, Jay walks home with me and Danny. I am quiet for most of the walk. Danny and Jay are talking about going to the basketball game at Northside High this weekend. When we get to the house, Danny goes inside. It's become a ritual now for him to make kissing noises every time he leaves me and Jay by ourselves.

I don't even bother to fuss at him. I just follow him into the house. "I'll be back," I tell Jay. I go inside. When I return, I have all the shopping bags in my hands. "I can't keep these," I tell Jay.

I wait for Jay to yell at me. Wait for him to say if I don't want his gifts some other girl will. But Jay doesn't say anything. He takes the bags and walks away. And I feel like my momma right now. I don't want anything I didn't earn the right way.

AND THE GLORY, FOREVER

. . . .

Serenity Evans
Mrs. Ross, 1st Period
Poetry Workshop

Identity Poem

SERENITY
Shy, respectful, hard-working.
Sister of one brother.
Lover of poetry, sleepovers,
and colored gel pens.
Who feels sad when people pass away,
and happy when she spends time
with her best friend.

Who needs her journal, her grandparents,
and peace of mind.
Who gives help at the soup kitchen.
Who fears death.
Resident of the City of Roses, a place where
windy roads lead to mountains and waterfalls.
A place where Douglass firs and pine trees
stand tall, kissing the sky. A place where
home is not a house
but wherever friends and family are.
EVANS

May is a busy month for Grandpa and Grandma. Besides the normal activities at the church, the Rites of Passage ceremony is tomorrow and Mother's Day is next week. Grandpa hasn't decided what he wants to do for Grandma. She keeps saying she doesn't want anything, but Grandpa insists. While Grandma is out grocery shopping for the soup kitchen, Grandpa talks to me and Danny in the kitchen, real low and soft, like what he's saying is top secret. "Here's some money so you and Danny can get your grandma something nice," Grandpa says to me. "And I want my change back," he says, smiling. I ask Danny what he wants to get.

"I don't know. Not perfume," he says. Grandma hates perfume. "And no flowers or anything like that," he adds.

We try to think of something special. "You want to go to the mall now?" Danny asks.

"I can't. Maria's on her way. We're practicing one last time for tomorrow."

Danny and I start brainstorming a list of gift ideas. Grandma comes home and Danny runs to hide the list. Grandma tosses her purse and keys on the coffee table. "Whew," she sighs. "I'm tired. I need a day off." Grandma yawns and sits on the sofa. She takes her shoes off and turns her ankles around in circles, stretching them. "My feet are so tired," she says. "Serenity, baby, when is Maria coming?"

"She's on her way," I tell her.

"Well, I guess I better get something on the stove for dinner."

My grandpa picks up the phone. "We're ordering pizza tonight."

"James, I don't mind cooking—"

Grandpa has already dialed. "Hello, ah, yes, I'd like to place a delivery order," Grandpa says.

Grandma chuckles to herself, stretches out on the sofa, and falls asleep by the time the pizza arrives.

When Maria gets to the house, we eat dinner and drink so much soda we are too full to practice or do anything else but lie on my bed and talk. "So," I ask. "How are things with your mom?"

"Things are better," Maria says. "Not perfect, but better. Miguel moved out, so that's good."

"Are you still going to Mexico for the summer?" I ask.

"Yeah. I can't wait to see my grandma and my aunts, uncles, and cousins," Maria tells me.

"When do you leave?"

"The day after school gets out," Maria says. "I'm going to bring you something back," she tells me. "Next summer, we should ask if you can come with me."

"Yeah. We should," I say.

Maria and I change into our night clothes. "I invited Jay to come tomorrow," I tell Maria.

"You think he will?" Maria gets in my bed.

"I don't know." I turn the lights out.

We lie in bed trying to go sleep but we keep talking. "What are you going to do this summer?" Maria asks.

"Grandma says I can take poetry classes at the community center," I tell her. "And I've been thinking about rearranging my room. I want to change it, you know, make it look different before we start high school in the fall."

Maria gives me all kinds of ideas about how I should change things around. We talk about a new color of paint and new bedsheets. I hear my grandma walking to the foot of the stairs. "Girls!" my grandma shouts. "Go to sleep! It's late. Tomorrow is a big day."

We lower our voices. Maria says, "I can't wait to start high school."

"Me neither." I take the cover off because it's warmer

than I thought. "Do you think we'll stay friends through-out high school?"

"Of course. We're like family. We'll be friends for-ever." Maria is snoring soon after that and then morning comes.

· · · · · · ·

The church is packed with people to see the candidates for the Rites of Passage. All of us who are being promoted to Teen Disciples are sitting in the front row. I am between Maria and Karen.

Maria's name is called first. Mrs. Mitchell reads an introduction about Maria, tells how many community service hours she worked, and then calls Maria up to the platform. Maria takes the mike. I can tell she is nervous. We've rehearsed so many times, I am saying the scrip-ture with her as she recites it—Ecclesiastes 4:9–11: "Two are better than one because they have a good return for their labor. For if either of them falls, the one will lift up his companion. But woe to the one who falls when there is not another to lift him up. Furthermore, if two lie down together they keep warm, but how can one be warm alone?"

She did it perfectly. The congregation claps and says, "Amen." Maria explains why she chose this scrip-ture and what it means to her. She talks about Ricky and Danny and her friendship with me and she says that she's learned that friendship is important and that she thanks God for sending people in her life that she can count on.

Mrs. Mitchell is crying and the entire church is on their feet clapping. Maria closes with a song, and Mrs. Mitchell and my grandma hand her a plaque. Maria steps down and comes back to sit next to me. She whispers, "I'm so glad that's over. I was so nervous."

"You did great."

"I didn't know we got plaques," I say. We look at it. The scripture Maria quoted is inscribed on the plaque in cursive writing. Maria turns it over and it has her full name inscribed on it. Under her name it says *Rites of Passage Ceremony, Restoration Baptist Church.* I think to myself that the first thing I'm going to do when I get home is look on the back of my momma's plaque.

Karen goes next, then Sabrina, then two more girls, and now it's my turn. My heart is pounding and my palms are sweaty. I get up to the podium and recite my scripture, Matthew 6:9–13, The Lord's Prayer. As I say it, everything I've been through flashes through my mind and I tell my story. When Mrs. Mitchell and Grandma hand me my plaque, I hold it close to my heart and go sit back down in the front row.

Mrs. Mitchell congratulates all of us and asks us to stand. Grandpa and a few other ministers say a prayer, and after the service is over we go to the fellowship room for a reception.

"It's official," Maria says. "We're young adults now."

Sabrina smiles. "No more youth Sunday school class."

Karen adds, "Or youth choir."

"Yeah, I get to sing in the teen choir," Maria says. "I can't wait to travel with them and open up for gospel concerts."

Mrs. Mitchell comes over to us and gives each of us a hug. "I'm just so proud," she says. "Remember, this means you have to be good role models for the middle school kids now."

We smile. I think all of us like the sound of that. When the reception is over, everyone goes their separate ways. "See you later," Karen says.

"Bye!" Danny and I get in the car with Grandma and Grandpa.

Danny takes a look at my plaque. "You two did really good," he says.

"They did great," Grandpa says.

On the drive home Danny falls asleep. The sun has set and I am starting to feel tired from all the excitement of the day. We ride past the park near my school. Jay is standing on the corner with two taller, older boys. His hands are in his pockets. He sees me passing by and I wave at him from the backseat. He tosses his head, saying what's up. I wonder if Jay found the envelope I left for him. I put the prayer I wrote for him in one of the bags. I think he'd like to know someone is praying for him.

When I get home, I rush to my room, take my momma's plaque off the wall, and turn it over. I don't know how it is I never looked at it before, or why Grandma never told me, but here it is—my momma's name with the words *Rites of Passage Ceremony, Restoration Baptist Church* under it.

I hang my plaque on the wall, to the right of my dresser. My momma's is to the left side. I think no matter how I rearrange my room, I will never take those down.

AMEN

· · · · · · · · · · ·

Serenity Evans
Mrs. Ross, 1st Period
Poetry Workshop

Ode: *a poem that gives tribute to something*
or someone. Write an ode about something you
love.

Ode to Cake

You're always there on my birthday,
And most holidays too.
No matter how good dinner is,
I save a place in my tummy for you.

I sometimes forget all the painful things
You've been through.
The beating, mixing, and baking
Just so I can taste you.

You're perfect plain,
Or with frosting on top.
I like you with ice cream.
I like you a lot.
There are many desserts I love to eat.
But a homemade cake is my favorite sweet.

It's Mother's Day weekend and it's taken hours for
Grandpa to convince Grandma to leave the house for the
afternoon. Her cookbooks arrived yesterday and he's been
hiding them in the basement. He'll be taking them to
local bookstores and to the street fair next week, but first
he wants to present her with one—make it special.

"Okay, your grandma will be back soon. Are you
almost finished?" Grandpa asks me and Danny.

"Almost," we say. Our gift to Grandma is giving her
a day off. When her cookbooks arrived, I picked out one
of the recipes, and Grandpa took me to the store to get
all the ingredients. I've been cooking most of the afternoon. The kitchen is hot and there are pans and pots
all over the countertop. When Grandma cooks, she keeps
everything so neat, but somehow I've made a mess of

things. Danny and I clean it all up and put the food on the serving trays. We set them on the dining room table.

Grandpa dims the lights. Lit candles sit on the table making pretty patterns on the tablecloth. Danny sets the table with Grandma's best dishes. I take the bread out of the oven.

"It looks beautiful," Grandpa says. "Your grandma is going to be so surprised."

I look at the table, making sure everything is perfect. The salad, pasta, sauce, and garlic bread are all on the table. Grandpa even bought sparkling cider and nice glasses. We set Grandma's cookbook on her chair. Grandpa has slid his gift to her in the front flap—a weekend of rest at a bed-and-breakfast.

"They're here," Danny says. He's looking through the curtains in the living room. "Erica's car just pulled up."

"Okay, just a minute, just a minute. Don't let them in yet." I run into the kitchen and get the red velvet cake.

"Hurry up!" Danny says.

I put the cake on the buffet table next to the vase of roses. "Okay, I'm ready."

RED VELVET CAKE RECIPE

. . . .

Ingredients
    2 ½ cups all-purpose flour
    1 ½ cups granulated sugar
    1 teaspoon baking soda
    1 teaspoon salt
    1 tablespoon unsweetened cocoa powder
    1 ½ cups vegetable oil
    1 cup buttermilk, at room temperature
    2 large eggs
    2 tablespoons red food coloring
    1 teaspoon white distilled vinegar
    1 teaspoon vanilla extract
    Cream cheese frosting
    Crushed pecans for garnish

Preheat the oven to 350 degrees F.
    Lightly oil and flour two 9-inch-round cake pans.
    In a large bowl, sift together the flour, sugar, baking

soda, salt, and cocoa powder. In another large bowl, whisk together the oil, buttermilk, eggs, food coloring, vinegar, and vanilla. Mix the dry ingredients into the wet ingredients until a smooth batter is formed.

Divide the cake batter evenly among the prepared cake pans.

Place the pans in the oven. Bake for 30 minutes.

Remove the cakes from the oven and let cool completely.

Cream Cheese Frosting

1 ½ cups cream cheese, softened
¾ cup unsalted butter, softened
1 teaspoon vanilla extract
3 cups sifted confectioners' sugar

In a mixing bowl, beat the cream cheese, butter, and vanilla together until smooth. Add the sugar and beat on low speed until incorporated. Increase the speed to high and mix until very light and fluffy. Store in the refrigerator until somewhat stiff, before using.

To frost the cake

Place one layer, rounded-side down, on a cake stand. Spread cream cheese frosting over the top of the cake. Top with the remaining layer, rounded side up, and frost the remainder of the cake. Sprinkle pecans on top.

ACKNOWLEDGMENTS

If there is such a thing as generational blessings, I pray that I have inherited the strength and faith of my brother and sisters, Roy, Cheryl, Trisa, and Dyan. You've been listening to and reading my stories since I was seven years old. Thank you for your unwavering support.

I am fortunate in that I grew up surrounded by many caring adults. Two of them are my godparents, Reverend Felton Howard and Mrs. Thelma Howard. When you left this earth, you left behind lessons of walking by faith and not by sight, lessons of perseverance, of compassion, and of grace. Thank you.

For reading first drafts and baking a lovely red velvet cake: thank you, Jonena Welch. Your friendship has rescued me countless times. My sincere gratitude to Chanesa Hart, Cherise Frehner Mahoney, Jemima Vanwalk, Donna and Russ Calahan, Fernando Ibarra, and Michael Smith. Thank you for reading excerpts and giving feedback and for cheering me on.

I am deeply thankful for my writing instructors at The New School: Nancy Kelton, Sharon Mesmer, Julia Noonan, Sue Shapiro, and Catherine Stine. Catherine, thank you for bringing me into your writing group: Maggie, Holly, Jonas, Courtney, and Bernard, your critiques were invaluable.

And much appreciation to my agent, Ethan Ellenberg, and my editor, Victoria Wells Arms, for wisdom and guidance.

© NAACP

RENÉE WATSON is the *New York Times* bestselling and Newbery Honor– and Coretta Scott King Award–winning author of *Piecing Me Together*, *This Side of Home*, *Betty Before X*, co-written with Ilyasah Shabazz, and *Watch Us Rise*, co-written with Ellen Hagan, as well as two acclaimed picture books: *A Place Where Hurricanes Happen* and *Harlem's Little Blackbird*, which was nominated for an NAACP Image Award. She is the founder of I, Too Arts Collective, a nonprofit committed to nurturing underrepresented voices in the creative arts. She grew up in Portland, Oregon, and currently lives in New York City.

www.reneewatson.net

@reneewauthor

DON'T MISS RENÉE WATSON'S OTHER POWERFUL FICTION FOR YOUNG ADULTS.

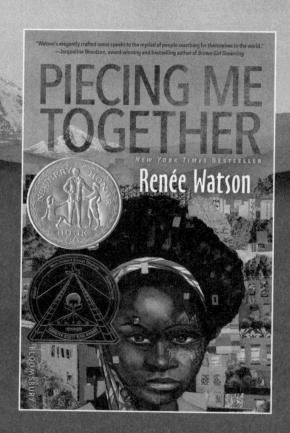

"Watson's elegantly crafted novel speaks to the myriad of people searching for themselves in the world."
—Jacqueline Woodson, award-winning and bestselling author of *Brown Girl Dreaming*

PIECING ME TOGETHER

NEW YORK TIMES BESTSELLER

Renée Watson

NEWBERY HONOR BOOK

BLOOMSBURY

Be bold.
Be brave.
Be beautiful.
Be brilliant.
Be (your) best.

A powerful story about a teen girl striving for success in a world that too often seems like it's trying to break her.